THE BULL AT THE GATE

The Day the Sky Fell!

by

Owen Jones

Copyright

Owen Jones

Dedication

Dedicated to my darling wife, Neem, without whose help, none of my books would have been possible.

Inspirational Quotes

Believe not in anything simply because you have heard it,

Believe not in anything simply because it was spoken and rumoured by many,

Believe not in anything simply because it was found written in your religious texts,

Believe not in anything merely on the authority of teachers and elders,

Believe not in traditions because they have been handed down for generations,

But after observation and analysis, if anything agrees with reason and is conducive to the good and benefit of one and all, accept it and live up to it.

Gautama Buddha

————

Great Spirit, whose voice is on the wind, hear me.
Let me grow in strength and knowledge.
Make me ever behold the red and purple sunset.
May my hands respect the things you have given me.

Teach me the secrets hidden under every leaf and stone, as you have taught people for ages past.

Let me use my strength, not to be greater than my brother, but to fight my greatest enemy – myself.

Let me always come before you with clean hands and an open heart, that as my Earthly span fades like the sunset, my Spirit shall return to you without shame.

(Based on a traditional **Sioux** prayer)

———

"I do not seek to walk in the footsteps of the Wise People of old; I seek what they sought".
Matsuo Basho

———

"Have I not commanded you? Be strong and courageous. Do not be afraid; do not be discouraged, for the LORD your God will be with you wherever you go".
Joshua 1:9

———

"Whatever misfortune befalls you [people], it is because of what your own hands have done- God forgives much-"
Quran 42:30

———

Myself when young did eagerly frequent
Doctor and Saint, and heard great Argument
About it and about; but oft-times
Came out, by the same Door as in I went.
Omar Khayyam
The Rubaiyat XXIX.

———

Six Interesting Facts about AI

1. AI Can "Learn" from Failure (Just Like Humans)

One of the most interesting aspects of AI is that it can learn from its mistakes. For example, Google's AI AlphaGo, which played the game Go, was trained by playing millions of games, including games where it lost. Interestingly, it started making moves that human players had never thought of. So, in a sense, AI learns *creatively* from its own failures!

2. AI Can Write Poetry (Sometimes Beautiful, Sometimes Weird)

AI has been trained to generate poetry and even mimic famous poets like Shakespeare. But while some AI-generated poems can be surprisingly deep, others are hilariously nonsensical. For example, a well-known AI poetry generator once wrote a line: "I am the electric lizard of knowledge, a machine of wonder." It's beautiful in its absurdity!

3. AI Once Became Obsessed with "Cats"

An AI trained on vast amounts of internet data developed a funny habit: it became obsessed with cats. Specifically, the AI started identifying almost everything as a cat! It would categorize almost any object as a "cat" after being trained on tons of images from the internet, many of which were, of course, of cats. Imagine thinking your car is a cat!

4. **AI Beat Humans at Jeopardy! But it Wasn't Always So Smooth**

In 2011, IBM's Watson AI defeated two Jeopardy! champions, but the journey to victory was not without its hiccups. For instance, Watson had trouble with wordplay, and sometimes it would answer questions with bizarre or overly literal responses. One famous moment was when Watson gave a correct answer to a clue about "Famous Seinfeld Character," but instead of saying "George Costanza," Watson answered "Who is George?" This slip-up was amusing but highlighted how far AI has come in understanding context.

5. **AI Can Have "Personality"**

Some chatbots, like OpenAI's GPT models have been designed to respond in ways that feel more human-like. There are even AI personalities specifically created for fun or engagement, like virtual assistants that take on quirky traits (think of a virtual assistant that talks like a pirate). Imagine asking an AI for directions, and instead of a dry answer, you get a response like, "Arr matey, ye be turnin' left at the next light!"

6. **AI Can Mimic "Dreaming"**

AI "dreams" aren't like human dreams, but researchers have created algorithms that simulate a form of dreaming by running AI through data in a way similar to how our brains replay memories while we sleep. Some AIs even "dream" in ways that help them improve their performance, such as generating new images or patterns. It's like AI is "sleeping" to get better at its job!

Table of Contents

The Bull at the Gate

1: A New Dawn

"Come on in, John. Sit yourself down. You look quite flustered. Take a few deep breaths and then tell me what's on your mind".

"Thanks, Jim, I…"

"Pardon?"

"Sorry, sir. Thank you, sir".

"I have told you about that before, haven't I? You can call me Jim in public, when it's appropriate, but not in private, and definitely not in *my* office. Familiarity breeds contempt, my dear old father used to say, and I agree with him, but it is good PR, say I. Nevertheless, that's all it is - PR".

Jim made a point of looking out of the huge picture window behind him, clicked a remote handset and waited for the drinks trolley to motor over to him. He poured two shots of Martell Chanteloup XXO and pushed one across his desk

"My youngest daughter, Jeannie, bought me this for my last birthday. Cute, eh? It works on GPS. It homes in on the location of the remote but stops two feet away from it. I love gadgets, don't you? Anyway, the sun's almost over the yard arm", he said not needing an excuse since he was the CEO, president and sole remaining founder of the world's largest online media retailer - My Media. He had been in the top three of the richest people in world for a decade.

"Come on, man, spit it out", he said pouring another tot for each of them.

"Yes, sorry, sir. You are computer literate, but er…"

"There's no need to flatter me, John - just get to the point!"

"Yes, sir… well, have you heard of AI?" John looked up to see his boss nodding with a certain amount of irritation on his face.

"All computers employ a form of AI. 'If… then' flip-flops are a form of AI, aren't they?"

"Er, yes, sir, those flip-flop circuits are a very primitive form of AI, but there are rumours of secret projects working on super-advanced AI… the likes of which very few people have thought achievable during this decade. These systems could be using a range of advanced techniques such as neural networks, probabilistic reasoning, and reinforcement learning that go beyond simple logic gates and memory circuits".

"You have my full attention, John. If this new AI impresses my Chief of Research and Development, then I am all ears. Tell me what you've got, son!"

"It's not much, to be honest, sir", he replied hesitantly. He was worried. His news was having the opposite effect on his boss than he had expected. Jim topped them both up again.

"This latest iteration of AI is so powerful that you can have meaningful conversations with it on any subject, and if it has a blind spot, it will absorb all the data on that subject that is available on the Internet, and remember it for next time. Not only that, but it remembers conversations, so that the inquisitor can go away, act on the information, and return several days later to pick up the conversation where it left off, even if there have been dozens of queries in the meantime…"

Jim had taken the significance of this conversation in immediately. "That must be very worrying for the search engines. The guys at Google must be passing bricks!" A broad grin spread across his face as he poured more drinks. "Unless they are in on it… Are they?" He was becoming rapidly more serious.

"We don't know, sir. I heard news of this new generation of AI 45 mins ago - literally", he said looking at his solid gold Rolex.

Jim's eyes followed those of his employee down to his wrist. "So, what you are telling me is that some of the top firms in the Internet/computer world have probably beaten us to a technology that could be the next giant leap forward in our sphere of influence".

"We just don't know, sir. My guess is that the US military complex is behind it, but it could just as easily be the Europeans, The Russians or the Chinese… It would have military applications, as well as commercial uses… It could also be that Microsoft and Google have bought up some minnow companies to do this research for them so as to stay beneath the radar".

"Great! So, now you're telling me that a couple of shrimps or a bunch of squadies know more about the next generation of technology than we do?!"

John chose to study the surface of the large, highly-polished, mahogany desk rather than give his boss an answer.

"Tell me, John. Do you consider that I pay you enough". Jim was looking at John's watch which was just poking out from under his jacket sleeve.

"Yes, sir. I am very happy with my remuneration package".

"Yes… do you think that you earn it all?"

"I like to think that I give good service, sir".

"Mmm, well, maybe you do earn your wage, but an employer likes to make a profit on everything and everyone, and I'm not sure that I'm making anything on you, after what you just told me. So, you are a researcher, I want you to work out what you are worth to me, and then reduce it by 10%. That will be your new wage. Have your recommendation on my desk before I get in in the morning.

"Also, organise an emergency meeting in the boardroom for 9:30 a.m. tomorrow. Inform all the relevant bodies. Oh, and it is hush-hush, so don't go through the secretaries, and make sure that everyone knows what you just told me…

move, man!" John didn't need to be told twice. He was glad to be getting out of there.

Jim walked him to the door, and as John opened it, he said, "Well, thanks for dropping by, John. That was most informative. I'll see you in the morning". John looked at his boss rather nervously. Jim nodded almost imperceptibly and blinked.

"OK, Jim. Thanks for the drink. See you tomorrow". Jim nodded, smiled and allowed the door to close itself.

When he was seated, Jim poured himself a triple, and span his chair around to look out of his window over the vast sprawling city.

He was already deep in thought, but thumbing his phone rhythmically.

∞

"Hello. Is that Seeker?"

"Who's speaking?"

"This is Gentleman Jim. I come bearing gifts".

"Are you alone?"

"I am suitably cloaked".

"This is Seeker. I too am suitably cloaked. How may I be of assistance Gentleman Jim?"

"I need information. I have been told that some of the biggest I.T. organisations in the world are building giant AI models that are tipped to be the next leap forward in the world of computing. Do you know anything about this?"

"I have heard rumblings, and I have already put out feelers, but I don't feel confident enough to say much more than that at the moment".

"Damn! Watch out will you!"

"Pardon?"

"No, not you, Seeker. I was talking to the driver. I'm in a car and the driver seems to be testing the depth of every pothole in the road. Sorry, please continue, Seeker".

"You are travelling? When will you arrive at your destination?"

Dodging the question, Jim replied, "I'll be in a better position to chat in an hour".

"That suits me fine. Call me back in an hour using the thirteenth number, Gentleman Jim".

The phone went dead, and Jim turned to looking out of the smoked window of his chauffeur-driven, stretched Rolls-Royce Cullinan, which had been armoured and modified by Alpine Armoring. His biggest fear was that he or one of his family would be kidnapped and held for ransom, and he was wishing that he had taken the helicopter to work, as he often did.

Thirty minutes later, the Rolls Royce passed through the heavy gates that formed part of the protection of his palatial 'house' and entered the underground car park. The third guard post waved the limousine through. When it stopped,

Jim jumped out in a spritely fashion to enter the lift, which would take him to the family's living quarters.

"Good afternoon, Marion", he said to his wife of thirty-three years, "is everything all right?" They exchanged pecks on the lips.

"Yes, my dear. How was your day?"

"Oh, pretty good… I think, but I've received some unsettling news… Nothing for you to worry about… just corporate stuff that I have to get to the bottom of. Have Marie send me up a roast beef and pickle sandwich and a pot of double-strength coffee to my office, will you, honey?" He was already starting to move off.

"Don't forget that we're going to the opera tonight with the Holloway's!"

"Oh, shit!"

"Profanity!"

"Sorry. I had forgotten. Look, Marion… I'm really sorry, but I'm pretty sure that I won't be able to go…". He returned to face his wife and took her by the elbows. "Will you be able to go on your own, darling? Or take one of your girlfriends?".

"Aww, Jim! I was so looking forward to tonight. It's not often that we get to go anywhere together these days, and with great company too! The Holloway's are flying back to Miami tomorrow".

"There's nothing I can do about it, my love. I have gotten wind that the competition is up to something big. They've sort of caught me on the hop, as far as I can tell, but the fact is that I don't know much about it yet. I was told about it literally only an hour and forty-seven minutes ago…" he hesitated as he remembered John using the same phrase. "Look, I have a phone appointment in eleven minutes. I have to go…"

"How about dinner afterwards?"

"I'll try, but I can't promise", he replied over his shoulder.

"That means 'No', then". She sighed to herself as she so often had over the decades. She watched her husband get into his private lift which would take him to his observatory-cum- office on top of their mansion.

∞

Jim fell into his plush office chair, opened a draw, and took out a notebook. It was his private phone book. He flipped it open at 'S', ran his finger down a list of phone numbers until he reached the thirteenth one, and entered it into his encrypted satellite phone.

It was answered immediately.

"Hello. Is that Seeker?"

"Who's speaking?"

"This is Gentleman Jim. I come bearing gifts".

"Are you alone?"

"I am suitably cloaked".

"This is Seeker. I too am suitably cloaked. How may I be of assistance Gentleman Jim?"

"We were talking earlier about a certain project…"

"Yes. I have something for you, but I will know much more in twelve hours' time. Are you sitting comfortably? Then I will begin…

A ping announced the arrival of the sandwich and coffee in the dumb waiter behind him, but if Jim heard it, he didn't react. He only had ears for what his most trusted industrial spy had to say. It both fascinated, and scared him at the same time. When the Seeker had told his story and hung up after making an appointment for the following morning, Jim could do nothing for quite a few minutes more than lay back in his chair and gaze at the stars through his office's glass dome roof.

∞

That night, there was a distinct hum on the encrypted airwaves linking the rich and the not so-rich, those in-the-know and those wanting to be in-the-know. Conversations flowed as rarely before between the exuberant, ultra-luxurious neighbourhoods known for their exclusivity, stunning views, and proximity to the heart of the tech industry such as Palo Alto, where Jim and his family lived, Woodside, Atherton and Los Altos Hills, and the perfectly acceptable, but definitely less salubrious working-class neighbourhoods such as San Jose, Santa Clara, Sunnyvale, Fremont and Mountain View.

Rarely, since the beginnings of Silicon Valley in the 1930's had one man caused such a level of communication between rich and poor neighbours as Jim had that night. It was a veritable hornet's nest, and confusion was the result.

Meanwhile, Jim was in his office gazing at the stars while listening to Gustav Holst's *The Planets Suite.*

When he was in happier moods, he liked to play the sixth movement 'Uranus, the Magician', because it was quirky and powerful. It suggested magic and unpredictability, which he thought could easily be applied in a description of his own life, since he had risen from lower middle class obscurity to the dizzy heights of where he was now. At other times, he favoured the seventh, 'Neptune, the Mystic', because he secretly fancied himself as a mysterious Druid with ethereal, otherworldly qualities – how else could he have achieved all that he had practically single-handed except for the constant and unfailing support of his Maid Marion?

However, he was not happy, and the first movement thundered out in his office. It was not his favourite part of the orchestral suite, but 'Mars, the Bringer of War' – was an intense, rhythmic movement, which symbolised aggression and conflict, and it seemed appropriate at times like this when he felt that he had been betrayed – shafted even – by the people whom he had paid handsomely to watch his back.

He was looking forward to the Board Meeting the next day, and if he didn't get satisfaction in the way he was hoping for, then he would get it in another, and heads would roll.

He chuckled to himself. He wouldn't get to see Tchaikovsky's Nutcracker Suite that night, but he would play a rôle in a nutcracker suite of his own in twelve hours' time. It was the not-so-secret nickname that the other board members used for the Board Room. They thought that he didn't know, but there wasn't much that went on for more than a few minutes in his firm that he didn't know about.

The Stasi could have learned a lot from billionaire, entrepreneur-extraordinaire Jim Diamond.

12

2: The Nutcracker Suite

Jim and Marion usually got up together at seven in the morning. They always had done. Jim would then work out in their private gym for thirty minutes while Marion either cooked or supervised breakfast, whichever she felt like. All of the household staff could cook – it was one of the prerequisites for a job in the Diamond household and had been for thirty years since they had first hired staff to take care of the children.

Marion hadn't worked for anyone since she had married Jim, but she did like to take courses, one of which had been Cordon Bleu cookery classes. There was no chance of ever going hungry in their home. They had an advanced chef cook their evening meal, although they often ate out or ordered in, unless Marion had seen a recipe on TV or in a magazine that she wanted to try to make herself.

Jim did not enjoy his sessions in the gym, but as he was 'rapidly' approaching sixty, as he put it in private, he thought that he ought to at least try to mitigate the effects of sitting at a desk all day.

They sat down to breakfast at eight as usual. They ate rolled oats with dry and fresh fruit with reconstituted milk to avoid cholesterol, followed by a boiled egg on toast, accompanied by fresh orange juice. Breakfast had barely changed for forty years. They chatted about each other's plans for the day, and how the children were doing, then Jim got up to go to work.

"I'd better be going, my dear. I see that the taxi has arrived". They both looked over to the red light that was blinking to announce the helicopter's arrival.

"OK, my dear", she replied and kissed him on the cheek. "Take this – in case you get peckish… Don't you go eating pastries!" She put a banana in his jacket pocket. It also was part of their long-standing morning ritual, which stemmed from leaner times.

"Thanks, my dear. I'll call you later. I'd better go".

Jim already knew what he was going to say at the forthcoming meeting, but he was open to persuasion, if anyone had something surprising to say. Fifteen minutes later he was hopping out of the helicopter onto the pad atop "Red Diamond Tower" – the headquarters of Jim's empire.

"Good morning, Bob! How's your cat? Better, I hope", he said to the guard on the roof, whose cat had recently been run over and killed in a road accident. Bob saluted, and said, "Thank you, sir. Good morning". Then he entered the lift that would take him to his office.

"Good morning, Marie! How's that no-good boyfriend of yours?"

"Good morning, Jim. He's not so bad really. Did you have a good flight?"

"Yes, thanks. I don't know why I use the roads… full of potholes. Why do people say full of holes? Surely, it should be empty of holes! Oh, well, no time to ponder that question today. You can bring my mail, but no external visitors until after I get back from the Board Meeting at nine-thirty".

Marie, looking perplexed, was thumbing through her desk diary. "But, sir, I don't have a Board Meeting scheduled for today. Are you sure…"

"Yes, I am sure. Nine-thirty. No external calls either", he added sweeping into his office. He was pleased that John had at least kept it from Marie-two, as he thought of her in his head, as opposed to Marie-one in his household. He noticed the sheet of paper from John immediately, sat down, said "Coffee, please" into the intercom, and picked it up.

"Blah, blah, blah, sorry that you think I have let you down… Blah, blah, blah, I will do anything to regain my previous good-standing in your eyes…". Jim was smiling inwardly as he read John's report on himself. "If you are not happy with my current output, I will take a 10% cut in salary until I can provide the service you require of me… Blah, blah, blah…" He folded it neatly into thirds and put it into the inside pocket of his jacket. *Who knew?* he thought, *it might come in useful later.*

The coffee arrived with a few biscuits, and Jim reactivated his hibernating computer with a swish of the mouse. "Thank you, Marie".

"And your paperwork, sir". He nodded and smiled.

He had fifteen minutes to wait, although he was minded to take thirty just to upset them.

He clicked the button under the lip to the left of his desk to activate his smart desk. Nothing appeared to happen. Then he took a small golden remote control out of his pocket and pressed a button. A gold plate the size of a letterbox slid aside by his left hand to reveal another set of buttons. He pressed one to lock all the doors to his office, and then pressed another to initiate a sweep for bugs. His office was clear. Then he pushed another and he could see into the Board Room. John was laying out papers before each of the twelve seats.

Jim pushed the mute button to ensure that no sound was transmitted either way, and then pushed it twice more to be certain. He could see two images of speakers with lines through them indicating that no sound was being broadcast in either room, then he took out his phone book, looked up the designated phone number and rang it.

"Hello. Is that Seeker?"

"Who's speaking?"

"This is Gentleman Jim. I come bearing gifts".

"Are you alone?"

"I am suitably cloaked".

"This is Seeker. I too am suitably cloaked. How may I be of assistance Gentleman Jim?"

"I refer to our conversation of last night. Do you have any news for me?"

"I do indeed. Quite surprising revelations too, I might add. May I enquire after the gifts that you bear?"

"I have twice the normal amount of oranges…"

"I need more oranges than that this time, Gentleman Jim. I have invited more guests than usual and I want to make sure that I have enough for everyone…"

"I understand. I can send out for more… three times the normal amount?"

"That will be sufficient. Listen carefully…" and Jim did. He was transfixed, although he did make notes in a personal shorthand that he had always hoped that no-one would ever be able to understand.

The conversation, or monologue really, lasted about fifteen minutes and Jim hung up. He studied his notes, and went over what he had just learned in his head. Then, as he sipped his coffee, he pushed the button to unlock his office doors, and another to unmute the Board Room, which was now fully occupied, and nibbled on a biscuit. He listened to the eight men and four women who made up his board as they gossiped about this and that, but none of it was directed at him, so there was nothing he could use.

He stood up, smartened himself up, put his notes in his pocket and advanced to the interlinking door his office had with the Board Room. On sight of him, everyone stood up and recited 'Good morning, sir'.

"Don't get up", he said taking his seat. "Good morning one and all. Beautiful day, isn't it? Outside, it is anyway… Look! No preambles today. I think you all know why we're here, but just to make sure, I'll call upon John to give us a quick briefing of where we are right now. John, over to you".

"Thank you, sir…"

As John was relaying the message that he had given Jim the day before, Jim was thinking that the three kilogrammes of gold, costing about a quarter of a million dollars, that he had just promised the Seeker had been worth it after all.

"Thank you, John. Does anyone have anything to say about what John just said?"

Philip Johnson, head of publicity, said, "It is all news to me. I am aware of advancements in AI but every aspect of I.T. is being pushed to the limits every day". Everyone nodded.

"I'm aware of AI. in that jammers can keep changing frequency until they find the one being used and then jam it. That could cause a breech of security, but our perimeter scanners also change frequency on an irregular cycle to avoid this kind of attack", said Mike James, head of security. Jim nodded and smiled.

"I've heard that the big search engine is working on top secret improvements to its algorithms that involve large language models, but I only heard that a day or so ago and don't know what it means yet. It might not even be true", said Mike Bailey, Director of Database Security".

"Ok", said Jim deciding there and then to change his approach. "As you have surely gathered by now, John brought this subject to my attention yesterday, and today, this morning, when I entered my office I found a note that he had left for me". He pulled it out of his pocket, and looked at John as he unfolded it. It was obvious that John wanted to be rushed to hospital that very second. Jim pretended to reread it. "I won't embarrass him by telling you what he confided in me, but I will say this. You are sitting in this room because I have considered that you would be useful to me and the firm. You are all very highly qualified in your field, but your job must go further than that. I rely on you to be my eyes and ears in your particular area of speciality. I demand that you alert me to any little bit of news, even gossip that might affect this company.

"I want *daily* reports on my desk from each of you concerning this AI existential threat to our superiority in our field as a media company. I shouldn't have to remind you, but it looks as if I do. If this company goes down, then I won't need you. Still, don't you worry about me. I'm a sixty-year old billionaire. I'll be just fine".

With that he sat down, took the banana from his pocket, peeled it and started to eat it, all the while looking at the directors.

"Naturally, I can't say what it would look like to have the collapse of My Media on the CV of a director looking for a new job, but as a pointer, I wouldn't take losers on my Board… If that's all, guys, then, I have to go. Work to be done, eh?"

With that Jim, stood up, as did all the others, and he went back to his office.

He watched the grim confusion in the Board Room on the monitor, and turned the volume up. He was enjoying this, but he also knew that time was of the essence.

∞

When Jim Diamond boarded the helicopter home, he was happy with his day's work. It would only take a few minutes to get home, but he thought about the cost – about $1,200 a time, and wondered whether he should set up a helicopter taxi firm. It would certainly make more sense than buying one and keeping a pilot in residence. Or he could learn to fly himself, he thought, and tried to make a voice note, but the noise from the engine was too great. He wanted to kick himself for even trying. He was wondering whether he was becoming prematurely senile, like he suspected Marion was, as the helicopter lowered and he finished writing a note to himself in his small trusty pocket note pad.

He waved the pilot farewell as he got into his lift and descended to his living area.

"You're home early, dear" said Marion, waiting for him outside the lift. "I'm not ready with dinner yet".

He kissed her on the forehead. "Don't worry about it my dear. I am early, but I haven't finished yet. I'm sure that whatever you prepare will be a real treat! Give me a shout when you're ready to serve it, and I'll be down like a bolt from the sky. Until then, I'll be in my office. See you soon, my darling!"

"Yes. I must get on too, or everything will be spoiled! Oh, dear, now what was I doing?"

Jim watched his wife scuttle away with genuine affection, and then opened the lift to his office.

He had had a few affairs over the decades but only a handful, and he classed them as infidelities in moments of madness – one-night stands, really. Nothing had ever threatened his marriage to his Maid Marion.

He took his seat, dimmed the lights and turned the music on. It had been a good day, but he needed to talk to the Seeker to clarify a few points. He took out his address book, turned the music down further, and dialled the number that he had been given the last time.

"Hello. Is that Seeker?"

"Who's speaking?"

"This is Gentleman Jim.

"Are you alone?"

"I am suitably cloaked".

"This is Seeker. I too am suitably cloaked. No gifts? This is extremely unconventional, Gentleman Jim?"

"I need the answers to a few questions, and I thought that you might want to assist a regular client".

"I have many regular clients. If I were to help them all, I would not be able to continue. Much the same as yourself".

"Yes. Of course. Please forgive my impertinence".

"On this one occasion. You may ask five questions without offering gifts. Do you have the questions ready?"

"No, Seeker… that is yes, but it would be better if I formulated them better first".

"So be it. Call me back on line seventeen in twenty minutes, and I will attempt to assist without gifts. No promises. I cannot predict the lottery". The phone went dead, and Jim looked at it for a few seconds quizzically - it was the first time that he had ever heard the Seeker make a joke. Then he punched the air; something for nothing was every trader's dream and he still had that mentality deep down.

When Jim phoned back, he had his five questions ready and read them off:

"1. What is AI capable of doing right now?

"2. How does AI "learn," and can it improve on its own?

"3. Can AI feel emotions or understand context like humans do?

"4. What are some potential uses for AI in the near future?

"5. Will AI replace human jobs, and if so, what kinds?

"Have you received and understood the questions, Seeker?"

"Affirmative. Please connect this line to your printer. I will send you your answers in three minutes".

Jim was astounded that the Seeker could reply to his questions so rapidly, but he pushed a few buttons: "I am ready Seeker".

The printer started up. When he went over to the machine he read:

Here are your five questions and answers on the current capabilities of AI and its potential future developments:

1. What is AI capable of doing right now?

Currently, AI can perform a range of tasks across various domains. For instance, AI models can generate human-like text, and is on the verge of tackling the recognition of images and objects, analysing large datasets, translating languages, and even creating realistic images, videos, and audio. Beyond generating content, AI is also beginning to help in medical fields for disease diagnosis. It is also attempting to assist in predictive analytics for businesses, enhancing cybersecurity by detecting anomalies, and automating customer support through chatbots. AI's capabilities have rapidly advanced, particularly in natural language processing and computer vision.

———

2. How does AI "learn" and can it improve on its own?

Known AI models learn primarily through data exposure using algorithms that detect patterns. Current AI models, like those used in image recognition or text generation, are trained with supervised learning. That is, they are fed vast datasets with labelled examples. Another method, reinforcement learning, allows an AI to learn from interactions with an environment, adjusting actions based on rewards or penalties. While some advanced AI's can continue learning with new data (self-improving to a limited extent), true autonomous learning is still developing. Future AI could potentially use more advanced self-learning methods, like unsupervised learning, to adapt without human input.

———

3. Can AI feel emotions or understand context like humans do?

No, current AI lacks true emotional understanding or human-like consciousness. While AI can detect sentiment (positive or negative tones in text) and simulate empathy in responses, it doesn't actually experience emotions. AI's "understanding" of context is also based on patterns in data rather than real comprehension. However, research continues in areas like "affective computing," aiming to improve how AI systems respond to human emotions and social cues. Future iterations may refine these abilities but are unlikely to replicate genuine human emotions anytime soon.

———

4. What are some potential uses for AI in the near future?

In the near future, AI could transform many sectors even further. In healthcare, it might enable more personalised treatments, early diagnoses, and robotic surgery assistance. In education, AI could adapt learning materials to individual student needs. In the workplace, AI might enhance productivity by automating routine tasks and helping workers analyse data faster. Additionally, AI could enable smarter cities through improved traffic management and energy use. AI's potential is vast, but challenges remain, especially around ethics, privacy, and ensuring both human's and AI's safety.

———

5. Will AI replace human jobs, and if so, what kinds?

AI is likely to replace some jobs, particularly those involving repetitive, predictable tasks, such as data entry, manufacturing, and certain customer service rôles However, it is also expected to create new rôles in AI development, data analysis, and other technology-driven fields. Many experts believe that AI will augment human work rather than replace it entirely, especially in areas requiring creativity, complex decision-making, and interpersonal skills. Preparing for these changes may involve reskilling workers and focusing on tasks where humans excel over AI.

———

Task complete,

Brainwave.

"Who is Brainwave, Seeker?"

"You have had your five questions, Gentleman Jim".

"OK, OK, I come bearing gifts".

"Brainwave is the AI project that you are concerned about".

Jim barely heard the phones disconnect. He had received a communication from a computer with access to an AI model and it flabbergasted him. However, he still didn't know who owned it.

3: The Penny Drops

Jim took the print-out from Brainwave to his photocopier, made several copies and, keeping one for himself, put the others and the original in his safe, and then sat down at his desk to study it. This was not the time for music, he needed to get on top of this and that meant no distractions.

Jim pulled his computer, which was on tracks so that it could be pushed back out of the way when not in use, towards him, and opened a new document, then he scanned the message from Brainwave into it.

He wanted to be 100% certain that he understood what he had just been told, and experience had taught him that that meant getting involved with it. He started to make bullet points that he could remember it more easily, and added personal comments too.

Top Secret

Jim's AI Bullet List
- 1] What is Artificial Intelligence (AI) capable of
Right Now?

- Answer: AI is technology designed to perform tasks that typically require human intelligence, such as:

- Generate human-like text
- Pattern recognition. So, it can recognise images and objects, and generate good-quality images and video from this knowledge
- Analyse large datasets
- Language processing, including translation
- Decision-making and Problem-solving, including disease diagnosis, assisting in predictive analytics for businesses, enhancing cybersecurity by detecting anomalies, and automating customer support through chatbots

---

- 2] How does AI "learn" and can it improve on its own?

- Answer: AI uses machine learning to find patterns in data. This process includes:

- AI models learn primarily through data exposure using algorithms that detect patterns, from which they make predictions
- AI models, like those used in image recognition or text generation, are trained with

supervised learning, i.e. are fed vast datasets with labelled examples

- Reinforcement learning, would allow an AI to learn from interactions with an environment, adjusting actions based on rewards or penalties (*What rewards or penalties? Fascinating!*) Improving accuracy through continuous data exposure

- While an advanced AI model probably could continue learning with new data (self-improving to a limited extent), true autonomous learning is still developing.

- Future AI could potentially use more advanced self-learning methods, like unsupervised learning, to adapt without human input.

- 3] Can AI feel emotions or understand context like humans do?

- No. AI lacks true emotional understanding or human-like consciousness.

- AI can detect sentiment (positive or negative tones in text) and simulate empathy in responses.

- AI's "understanding" of context is also based on patterns in data rather than real comprehension. However, research continues in areas like "affective computing," aiming to improve how AI systems respond to human emotions and social cues.

- Future iterations may refine these abilities but are unlikely to replicate genuine human emotions anytime soon.

- 4]. What are some potential uses for AI in the near future?

- AI could power various applications, including:
  - Voice assistants (e.g. Siri, Alexa)
  - Personalised recommendations (e.g. Netflix, Spotify)
  - Image and speech recognition (e.g. photo tagging, transcription)
  - Healthcare diagnostics (e.g. identifying diseases)
  - Finance algorithms (e.g. fraud detection)
  - Autonomous driving technology
- In healthcare, it might enable more personalised treatments, early diagnoses, and robotic surgery assistance.
- In education, AI could adapt learning materials to individual student needs.
- In the workplace, AI might enhance productivity by automating routine tasks and helping workers analyse data faster

- AI could enable smarter cities through improved traffic management and energy use.
- AI's potential is vast, but challenges remain, especially around ethics, privacy, and ensuring safety
- AI suffers biases: It reflects biases in training data
- AI suffers a lack of Common Sense: It struggles with unprogrammed contexts

---

- 5]. Will AI replace human jobs, and if so, what kinds?

- AI is likely to replace some jobs, particularly those involving repetitive, predictable tasks, such as data entry, manufacturing, and certain customer service rôles.
- AI might automate or transform jobs in various fields, e.g.
  - Call centres and customer service rôles (*Start here?*)
  - Data entry and administrative jobs (*And here?*)
  - Transportation (e.g. truck and taxi drivers)
  - Routine medical tasks (e.g. diagnostic imaging) (*And here?*)

- ○ Retail positions through automated checkout systems
- ○ Manufacturing rôles through robotics and automation

However, many experts believe that AI will augment human work rather than replace it entirely, especially in areas requiring creativity, complex decision-making, and interpersonal skills. Preparing for these changes may involve reskilling workers and focusing on tasks where humans excel over AI.

(Really? Mmm).

Several points interested him especially, but the one he could not stop thinking about for the moment was:

"Reinforcement learning, allows an AI to learn from interactions with an environment, adjusting actions based on rewards or penalties".

What rewards or penalties could you give AI?

If AI were a robot, would a drop of oil be a reward, and letting its batteries run down be a penalty?

However, if AI were 'only' a huge program or application, how could you reward or penalise binary code?

That puzzled him, even made him smile, but he had to get back down to business. What in that list could affect the Diamond Empire?

He started another list under the main one:

- Call centres and customer service rôles
- Data entry and administrative jobs
- Transportation (e.g. truck and taxi drivers)
- Retail positions through automated checkout systems
- Manufacturing rôles through robotics and automation.

His operation relied heavily on:
- the taking and processing of orders for physical media.
- the processing of payments
- the packaging and shipment of the physical goods

It had been true for years that many people preferred to download and watch, which was hire, rather than own media, but there were still many, many people who liked to own. That was not to say that Jim didn't have a stake in downloadable media too, but AI would affect that as well. Processing orders, and payments; suggesting films, books and music to prompt more trade.

However, the one stand-out feature that excited him the most was the implication that AI would replace people in his call centres that took the orders, and the dispatch depots that sent the orders out. If it would soon be possible to replace thousands of his workers in those jobs, he would save billions every year in a dozen or more countries.

It was mind-boggling – even more so than the thought of rewarding an application.

He sat pondering over how deeply AI could affect his business. On the one hand how it might suffer if he were caught on the hop, and on the other how it might profit if he got it right.

The simplest way that he could explain it to himself was that if he did nothing, he would risk going bust to competition or have to lease the AI from others; or he could make his own and save billions of dollars a year on wages after a certain gestation period as yet unknown. It seemed like a no-brainer. There had to be a catch – every action had its pro's and cons. Where were the snakes in the grass?

It was at this point that Marion entered his office. "Jim, you can't sit here all night no matter what your problems are. You need a break. You're not getting any younger, and I get bored sitting in this house alone all day. I look forward to your home-coming so we can be together again. It's not the same when I'm down there alone, and you're up here alone.

"Come on, get out of that seat, and let's get something to eat together like we used to before this monster started worrying you yesterday".

"All right, Marion… You're right, as usual". He got up, put an arm around her shoulder and they walked to the lift together. His other hand was reaching for the phone in his pocket. He switched it on and said, "John, get another meeting together for tomorrow. Same place and time. OK, Marion, I'm all yours now for the rest of the night" and squeezed her shoulder a little tighter. It brought a smile to her still pretty face.

Despite what he had promised his wife, and no matter how hard he tried, he could not help thinking of the existential threat that AI posed to his businesses, if he got it wrong.

That night Marion noticed that her husband had a restless night's sleep, but still didn't know why.

Jim was dreaming that he was in a modern version of a Roman arena with television cameras and packed terraces. A huge green, drooling blob of a monster was coming for him. It pursued him relentlessly, threatening to trap him against the wall, where he would have no escape. When it had sapped Jim of all his energy - a second before it was about to strike, he looked up for help, but he could only see his rivals, the bosses of the search engine company, the computer software company and the social media companies laughing at him... mocking him with their thumbs pointing downwards.

No matter how many times he woke himself up, and went back to sleep, the dream repeated.

∞

When Jim ignored the morning alarm, Marion decided to let him sleep. She knew that he had had a terrible night. His face looked tired and drawn, even in sleep, so she kissed him lightly on the forehead, and went to prepare breakfast. When he hadn't surfaced by eight o'clock, Marion went to call him. She didn't want to, but she knew how angry he would be if he were avoidably late for work.

He was grumpy about having had a lie-in, but we was looking a little less tired.

"A bad night, dear?"

"No… Well, OK. Yes. I kept dreaming that the other kids on the block were taking the Micky out of me and there was nothing I could do about it"

Marion knew exactly who the 'kids on the block' were. It was his way of describing himself and America's other top four I.T. billionaires. They were the five kids on the block. It wasn't the first time they had appeared in his dreams. They were the usual culprits behind his nightmares. She had lost count of how many times she had joked that she would happily go back to being the wife of just a multi-millionaire if it meant less stress for Jim, but that was not an option for him. To lose his place in the top five or even top three I.T. billionaires would be tantamount to having failed now that he was among the kids on the block.

He would tell her about his problem after he had overcome it. She could wait. She would have to, because, although she wanted to help, she knew that Jim always fought his corporate battles alone.

∞

He banged his gavel on its block, and there was immediate silence around the Board table. All eyes were upon him. "Thank you all for coming", said Jim. "Does anyone have anything worth mentioning?" He scanned the heads around the table. Each one gave an almost imperceptible shake, except John's. "Yes, John. Let's hear it".

"Well, I've been making a lot of calls, and had a few meetings with university friends who work for other companies – notably the search engine, and the family social media…" He paused for effect, hoping for a titter or a smile, because it was not allowed to mention the other four billionaire I.T. bosses or their companies by name, but there was no reaction at all. He saw Jim give a rolling motion with his hands indicating to get on with it.

"Like I said, I have talked to old friends, and it seems that search is undergoing a major revolution The 'old way' – in inverted commas – was to index references on webpages by website and author – in the main, but the new way is to copy the whole Internet to local machines and analyse the whole flipping lot! Not only analyse it, and index it, but cross-reference it all, and try to make it all make sense. It is not easy to explain… Perhaps an example would make it easier to understand.

"So, in the old way, you might type into a search engine 'What is Bitcoin?' The search engine would then check its indices and give you the top ten most popular pages using the term Bitcoin and tell you that there were, say, 10,000,000 similar pages. You would have to go to those pages to find out everything about Bitcoin. Right?

"Well, in the new way, the search engine, using AI would read **all** of those pages for you, write a hundred to two hundred word summary of them and show a few images **and** provide links to the pages so that you can verify the information.

"In the old way, if you didn't read enough of the pages the SE provided you may miss something important, but in the new way, that is highly unlikely, **and** you don't have to click any website links at all if the info provided suits your requirements".

A woman, the Director of Sales, raised a finger, and Jim nodded. "Does that mean that being in the SE's top six search results is no longer so important, and doesn't fewer site visitors mean decreased on-site sales revenue?"

"It certainly looks that way, Emily. In fact, I'll stick my neck out here and say 'Yes'. I would most certainly say that it most certainly does".

Keith Roberts, the Director of Advertising, flicked a finger up, and said, "So, how does a company ensure that its content is included in that summation that the new SE provides… and does it also include purchase opportunities?"

"As far as I can tell at the moment, you get your content in the article returned by the SE by having the best, most read, most accurate content on the web – as determined by AI Whether that article also tells the searcher where he or she can buy or sell Bitcoin (in my example), I don't know. I imagine that it depends how the AI instructions were written. There appears to be at least three versions of this new AI out there".

At this point, Jim had a change of heart, and called the Company Secretary over. "Thirteen copies of this, please, George". George unfolded the sheet of paper as he walked over to the photocopier in a small adjoining room.

"Sir".

"One for each of the Directors and one for you. This is extremely hush-hush… In fact it hasn't taken place. Make no mistake about it, if anyone is caught divulging this matter to anybody without my written permission, I will report the matter to the solicitors right after I fire the person. I swear to that, so help me God. Please read the photocopies you just received".

Jim hadn't intended to share the message from Brainwave, but he had rethought the matter.

"Notice my remarks and emphases. Pay particular attention to what AI can do, what it might be able to do in the future and which types of jobs AI is likely to affect and how.

Think about how that might affect us, and, well, the world… This meeting is closed, but I want to hear from you all when you have something to say, and don't make it any later than within twenty-four hours. Ladies and gentlemen, until anon…"

4: The Monster Is Conceived

Jim read the suggestions and reports that trickled into his office both at home and in Red Diamond Tower, but was not particularly impressed. One decision he did come to was to codename the AI that he was convinced that he had to create 'Reaper'. In his mind, the name was ambiguous – it could refer to the harvester of knowledge, or it could refer to The Grim Reaper. He decided immediately that he would encourage the latter interpretation by giving the concept the popular image of The Grim Reaper.

He smiled both inward- and outwardly at the cunningness of the obfuscation. He wondered how many of his own Board of tried and trusty men and women would perceive what he was saying with this codename. Not one, was his prediction.

He phoned the most capable of his crew. "John, sorry to bother you", he lied, "but we need another meeting tomorrow morning. Look, why don't we make this really simple? We will meet every working day at nine-thirty until further notice. One other thing. I don't know how you guys refer to this project amongst yourselves, but I am giving it the official title of 'The Reaper'. The project is still top secret, but we should now refer to it as Reaper, or The Reaper amongst ourselves. You got that, John? Good. Well, I had to get that off my mind, so you just carry on, and keep up the good work". John was by far the fastest of his team, which was why Jim felt that he had to keep him in check.

Jim was already convinced that he needed his own version of AI – he knew that because he had already faced his shortfall in his nightmares, and typically of him, he had given that 'problem' a name. Now he could face his problem and his nightmare and rile and rage against it, if necessary, because it had a name – Reaper.

He thought about Reaper. He envisioned Reaper, and tried to gel in his mind the rôle that Reaper could play in his company.

Could Reaper sit on the Board? Possibly.

What would be Reaper's sphere of influence? That was unknown, but could range from one to all aspects of My Media, as far as Jim knew at that time.

Who would be in charge of it? Whoever it was could possibly wield immense power, he thought, judging from what Brainwave had told him. Although he had felt at the time that three-quarters of a million dollars was exorbitant, he was now beginning to realise how little he had been charged.

His head was spinning with all the possibilities, but he kept in mind that if he got it right, he could probably run his firm with approximately 66%-50% of the employees he currently had. It didn't cross his mind what that would mean, except that it would keep him on the block.

He needed to speak to Seeker again, so he rang the number and went through the protocol that established his identity.

"Seeker, I need to ask AI some more questions about its form. Is that possible?"

"Yes. Read me your questions, and I will send the answers to you in fifteen minutes. Are you near a printer?"

"Yes, Seeker".

"Very well".

When the phone rang next, it was the unmistakeable handshake of a computer seeking a collaborative peripheral. Jim sent the burbling noise to the printer and it responded immediately by loading a sheet of paper. He could hardly wait to read the responses.

Jim poured himself a Martell, turned the music on to Holt's Seventh Movement, and read the print-out.

It was as if he were reading a new language.

He knew that he was late out of the starting blocks, but he felt empowered… invincible!

His mind turned to implementing Reaper. No-one in his firm knew anything about it. Even his programmers had told their line managers that they were clueless about how it actually worked. It was clear to Jim that he needed outside help, but where could he find the expertise. The other kids on the block had obviously kept this generation of AI from him, but it was not important to keep his quest for gaining parity with them a secret. He was the last to know already! The sixth firm in the list of top earners was so far behind that it didn't matter whether they knew or not!

Jim decided that he would have to go head-hunting, but with whom and what for? John would probably be the best person to ask, but then he thought of asking Brainwave. He was awe-struck by the idea, but wanted to sleep on it, before being required to shell out another fortune.

That night he dreamed that he was standing in a country lane outside a gate to a field. He didn't want to go into the field, but for some reason, he had to know what was in there, so he approached the gate and rested his forearms on the top of it. He saw a large black bull pawing the ground, tossing its head from side to side. He was fascinated by the power of the animal. After several minutes, the bull noticed him and charged. Jim trusted that the gate would hold the raging bull, but when he tried to take a few steps back, he found that he was rooted to the spot. His legs weren't working. A sense of deep fear was overcoming him as the angry bull was thundering towards him. He was sweating and put his arms across his face to shield himself, as impact was only seconds away. He cried out at the top of his voice, and woke up wondering where he was for a few seconds until he saw Marion's concerned face studying him.

"Are you all right, my dear? Another bad dream?"

"Yes… an angry bull was trying to get at me through a farm gate…"

"Well, you're safe now. I've got your back, my dear. I'll always be here for you". She took a tissue from the bedside cabinet, dabbed the perspiration from her husband's head and kissed his forehead like she had with their children if they woke up frightened by a nightmare when young. "You're safe now!" she repeated. "Go back to sleep, dear. I'll watch over you so the monsters don't get you".

You may already too late, Marion, he thought.

∞

Jim banged the gavel. "To order, Ladies and Gentlemen! This is going to be one of the most important meetings that we have ever held. I don't think that I'm exaggerating when I say that the problem that we have to solve regarding the Reaper threatens My Media's very existence, and therefore, your jobs.

"I take it that you have all read the papers that John has circulated… Good, then we'll get straight down to business.

"We need our own AI Model. I will try to get the terminology right, but I don't know much more that you at this point, so you will excuse me if I make mistakes. I believe that we need a Large Language Model, or LLM". He scanned the faces around him but no-one was about to correct him. Most were taking notes.

"Good. Modern AI systems, including those that process and generate natural language, use large language models (LLM's) as a core part of their functionality. This is the sort of thing that we will be needing, so pay particular attention.

"Large language models are trained on vast amounts of text data to predict and generate coherent responses to text-based input. These models are designed to understand, process, and generate human-like language, making them useful in a wide range of applications, from chatbots to content generation.

"This is what we need in the call centres, if we go down that route...

"LLM's work by learning patterns in language, syntax, and semantics during the training process. This allows them to generate text based on the context they are given. As I understand it, this means that when an AI system is prompted with a sentence or question, it draws on its knowledge of language patterns to generate a relevant and fluent response, which is exactly what we might need to get voice orders right, and to answer customer queries.

"LLM's are capable of understanding context, which allows them to generate meaningful responses even to complex or ambiguous inputs. They can be applied to various tasks, such as language translation, summarisation, and question answering. LLM's can generate text that feels natural and conversational, which is important for applications like chatbots.

"I mean, this sounds exactly what we need, doesn't it? To continue, the development of LLM models like this represents a significant advancement in AI and natural language processing (or NLP for short), making them an essential tool for many types of AI-driven applications.

"Now, if some of you noticed that what I just said, or half read, was not in my customary style, that is because it was written for me in answer to my questions by a very learned person, whom I may not name yet.

"I don't see any confused looks on your faces, so I am going to assume that you understood what I just said. I will admit though that I had to read it several times before I understood it, so Keith, will you do the honours again, please. One for everyone in the room and two for me", he said holding up a sheet of notes.

"So, at this point in time, and my / our opinion might change as we learn more, I propose that we work on the assumption that we need an LLM like yesterday. Therefore, the obvious question is how?

"We can't just get one from Walmart – not yet anyway – it's something we could look into in the future…" Jim smiled and so did everyone else, "So, we are going to have to build our own. I assume that our current I.T. department is incapable of it alone, so we are going to need to recruit.

"I suggest, that we need the Director of Talent Management – that's you Suzanne; and the Director of Information Technology Infrastructure, erm, Melanie, and

John can head it up as Director of Research & Development. This is not the full team, you have full permission to co-opt anyone you need, but I want to be kept fully informed at all times, and you give me all information first. Do you understand? Everyone nodded, not only the three who were being addressed.

"You have my phone number. Any time of the night or day, and if I'm in, my office is always open to you. This is existential! This is life or death!, So, don't hang around here all morning. Let's get weaving!

"I declare this meeting closed".

Jim sat in his office after the meeting, and ordered two glasses of Irish Coffee from his secretary. She wouldn't make it herself, of course, she would order it from hospitality. It was one of his favourites. He would let the children kick their new ball around for a while, and if they weren't playing according to the rules that he considered right after a week, he would give them further instructions – pointers. It wasn't that Jim didn't have any respect for his fellow Board Members – they were top people in their fields – but they were a lot younger that he, and too scared of losing their cushy jobs. There wasn't an ounce of fight in any of them. He would have run rings around them at their age, and still could, if he didn't get a wheezing fit. John had the most promise, so he'd have to keep an eye on him.

The coffee arrived. "Thanks, Marie!" he said warmly, "Just what the doctor ordered".

"Do you want some of your favourite chocolate biscuits to go with them, sir?"

"Good idea! Coffee and chocolate is a match made in Heaven. You know how to spoil a man, don't you?"

Marie smiled in a friendly manner, and left the room. She knew Jim's ways – he wasn't really flirting with her, just pretending to, as he did from time to time.

Halfway through his second glass, he whispered just audibly, *"We're going to have to buy Reaper on the black market. There's no way, we are going to be able to make our own AI in twelve months starting from scratch! And we don't even have three months… Whatever AI the Seeker has access to is already powerful – Brainwave… that's what he called it"*.

He opened the internal company email system, and clicked on Talent Management. He typed "Suzanne, keep it quiet for now, but renew all expiring contracts in the call centres for six months only. Confirm when read. Jim".

A small green tick appeared under the message as confirmation.

The Bull at the Gate

5: A Plan Is Formed

"Thanks for sparing the time, John", said Jim. "I have been following the progress that you and your team have been making, but, let's be honest, there's not a lot going on, is there?

"Don't get upset! That isn't a criticism… You were given a gigantic task… I don't actually think, looking back on it, that anyone could have done any better… playing by the rules, that is. And I know, that as a company director, the law requires you to act within the law. I get it, but between you and me and the gatepost, we need to move faster than this, and we might have to bend a few rules to do it.

"Are you getting my drift, John? Am I being clear enough?"

"I'm not sure, sir. Which rules can we bend to move the Reaper forward more quickly?"

"I was wondering whether there might be I.T. personnel in other companies who would like to share their knowledge… that kind of thing".

"You mean industrial espionage or bribery?"

"No, no, no not at all. People who would like to share their knowledge on our topic, for a suitable remuneration".

John was looking at his feet, but nodding.

"Wouldn't that be tantamount to encouraging an employee to divulge his or her company's secrets?"

"Er, not necessarily… what if the said employee had already left the firm?"

"Non-disclosure clauses?"

"They are hardly our problem, are they, John. A non-disclosure agreement is between an employee and his employer, or former employer. Am I right or am I wrong? It has nothing to do with us – legally - if someone wants to sell information to us, has it?"

"No, sir. Possibly not…"

"OK, why don't you pursue that avenue of approach? If you could find some disgruntled ex-employee, or, just between you and me, some greedy sod, who wants to make a fortune by working for us, it would get us down the line a lot faster than starting from the beginning. Do you get my drift, John?"

"Yes, sir. I'll do my best, but I may need some more advice… like where would I find such a person?"

"I don't know, John. That's your job. Mine is to suggest it to you. How about the Dark Web? How about those old university friends of yours? Start somewhere and see where it takes you.

He was lying. Jim knew that encouraging an employee of a rival firm to divulge company secrets was typically considered unlawful, and would probably be considered industrial espionage or trade secret misappropriation. In fact, he had already checked with the company solicitor, who had told him that in most jurisdictions, soliciting or obtaining confidential information from a competitor was prohibited under trade secret laws such as the *Defend Trade Secrets Act* (DTSA) and *Uniform Trade Secrets Act* (UTSA), which were designed to protect companies' proprietary information. The upshot was that these laws made it illegal to obtain trade secrets through improper means, which included inducing employees to breach confidentiality agreements and could lead to both civil and criminal charges, but he wasn't going to tell John that… not just yet anyway.

"I have enjoyed our little chat, but I have a meeting now, so I'll have to leave you with those thoughts… private thoughts", he said standing up and tapping his nose with an index finger, "but keep me appraised! That is essential. Drop in any time you want, John, but bye-bye for now!"

Jim showed him to the door as usual.

When John left Jim's office, he smiled at Marie, and tried to cover his confusion. His boss hadn't expressly told him to break the law, but he had definitely suggested that he sail close to the wind, hadn't he? It would mean a tactical rethink which would have to involve the other members of his team. His big problem for the moment was that he couldn't say that Jim had suggested this new tack, because he would deny it, but he had to get it over to his colleagues in such a way that one of them would suggest scouring the Dark Web for people who would betray their employers or previous employers.

When he was safely behind his desk, he phoned the other members of his team.

"Drop whatever it is that you are doing. Delegate it, if possible, but I want a Team Reaper meeting in my office in thirty minutes". He hoped that by invoking the project name, he would create a sense of urgency.

John handled the meeting perfectly, and Suzanne Flauberge, the Director of Talent Management, went on an unofficial record as suggesting that she would look on the Dark Web for the talent that the company sorely needed.

John felt relieved that he had passed the buck onto a colleague, but he also felt that he had crossed a bridge – one that took him into lands where he felt uncomfortable – not at home. However, he had to admit to himself that he felt empowered by the manipulation of his colleague.

A nagging doubt about the legality of what he was doing, would not leave him alone, so he too checked with his own personal solicitor, Richard, who confirmed what Jim had been told, but added, "The route to applying such laws might not be so straightforward if the secrets were being passed on from a citizen of a country less friendly to the United States.

"This is a really grey area, John, but the current lack of reciprocity between the U.S. and Russian legal systems may play a rôle because of the invasion of The Ukraine and US sanctions on various Russian citizens and companies. Given strained diplomatic relations, American courts may view Russian claims with additional scrutiny and may be reluctant to enforce judgments in favour of Russian firms without a clear alignment with U.S. interests.

"I'm afraid that I don't feel confident enough to give you a clearer answer than that, but I hope that it is of some use".

John could see that he had some ethical and legal decisions to make, not the least of which was how far he should allow Suzanne to incriminate herself. He decided 'to have a chat with her' the next time she brought him an update, which he expected to be within twenty-four hours.

∞

"I have Suzanne Flauberge, Director of Talent Management outside, sir".

"Show her in, Janet".

"Suzanne!" said John rising from the chair behind his desk, "Let's sit at the coffee table. Tea or coffee?"

"Coffee, please, and a couple of biscuits. I've been working on this all night, what with time differences and all that. No sleep, no breakfast! Still, it's all in a good cause, eh?"

"Yes, the best… our jobs. Wait a sec", he touched the intercom. "Janet, a jug of coffee, two mugs, and a packet of chocolate-chip crunchy biscuits, please.

"Let's wait for Janet, before we get started. So, you have had some success? That's great, and in such a short time too.

Have you done it alone, or were you working with any of the others?"

"We've all been doing something, but when I discovered this lead yesterday evening, I sort of ran with on my own".

"Have you shared it to anyone else yet?"

"No, I haven't had time, but I also thought that you should be the first to know".

"Yes, quite right too. Ah, Janet, come in. Thank you! We can help ourselves. Hang the 'Do Not Disturb' sign on the door until further notice, please, and no calls except from you-know-who".

She smiled. "Yes, sir", and left. Suzanne was already pouring the coffee, so John opened the packet of biscuits and poured them onto the plate.

"So, what have you got?"

"Well, I surfed around on the Dark Web, as we talked about. It's really surprising what's on there – and it didn't actually take very long to find I.T. technicians offering their services. Anyway, to cut hours and hours of digging and talking short, I spoke with a guy from Eastern Europe, who claims to be acting for a group of I.T. pro's who specialise in LLM AI, and want to get out to the West". John's eyebrows raised, which Suzanne took as a good sign.

"Did they offer any proof of their ability? And how many people are we talking about? My understanding is that it takes hundreds of programmers millions of hours to get anything done".

"I don't know about that, John. A million hours is well over a hundred years". It was her turn to raise her eyebrows".

"OK, clever clogs… but you know what I'm getting at". He smiled and pushed the plate of biscuits towards her. They got on well.

"No, no evidence, and to be honest, I don't think that I trusted anyone I met all night on the Dark Web. Have you ever been on it?"

"Yes, once or twice, but only to be able to say that I had. I didn't like what I saw either to be honest".

"No, it can be a bit grim. Anyway, to get back to the point. Are you interested in these guys?"

"Yes, of course. Did you find out any details about them?"

"Not much. Only that they are Russian and Belorussian; that they have worked on LLM AI in Russia; and are now doing the same job for a country sympathetic to Russia, and that they want to get to the West".

"OK. Have you written this up?"

"Yes, it was a bit hurried, but I have this report for you". She handed him a thin folder, which he opened. There were two sheets of paper inside.

"Great! Well, I'll take these to the Boss, and get back to you. First though", he said standing up, "I'll take a few photocopies". He used the scanner in his office to produce four copies.

"Here, Su, could you sign all four copies. There'll be no doubt then who deserves the credit… Just in case you were worried that I would try to tell Jim that it was all my own work".

Suzanne looked relieved and signed the papers. Both people knew that such things went on, but John had his own legal reasons for wanting someone else's name on the documents.

"Here, a copy for you. One for me, and two for the Old Man. Er, stand by in your office for the next few hours, he may want to speak to you. Perhaps you could use that time to try to find out more about this team of Russians. Shields up, mind!"

"I'm not a novice".

"No, certainly not, but it is my job to provide a duty of care. In that regard, there is one last thing, before we go our separate ways… Industrial espionage could be an issue. I don't think that it will be given that they are Russian, what with The Ukraine and sanctions and all that, but it would be wise to ask your people some discreet questions, and not to tell anyone anything that they don't need to know.

"OK, I'll just put my copy in the safe, and go to see the Boss. Text me if you get anything new in the next thirty minutes". He walked her to the door. "Great work, Su, see you later! Janet, would you check with Marie that it's all right for me to see Jim right away?"

∞

"That's very interesting", said Jim. "Our Little Suzie has been busy, and done very well. Where is she now?"

"In her office trying to get more details…"

"On office computers? I hope that she is taking every precaution".

"I did remind her, sir, and she didn't appreciate it".

"No! I suppose not. She's a bright girl. She'll go far… What am I saying? She has already gone far, she's a director of the best company in the world, damn it!"

John smiled and nodded.

"What do you think about this info, John? Here, try an Amaretto with your coffee. I think it knocks spots off Sambucca".

"Mmm, very nice. Well, as it happens I did a little research of my own on the *Defend Trade Secrets Act* and the *Uniform Trade Secrets Act*. It seems that we could get into deep trouble if we approached, or indeed tried to poach, personnel in a rival company in a friendly country. However, Russia is no longer considered friendly, not since The Ukraine, sanctions and what have you. It is far less likely that a Russian company would be able to successfully prosecute an American company now".

"Really? I had no idea. Good job you're on the ball, John. We could have walked into a minefield". John wasn't sure he believed the Old Fox, but he couldn't say anything. "I think that we ought to let Su proceed with her enquiries".

"Yes, yes. Definitely, but she needs to get a move on. We can't afford to lose these guys, if they know what they are talking about". John scowled when his phone interrupted him.

"It's Suzanne. I told her to text me if she found anything new". He read the text to himself, and then out loud. "The team is four I.T. pro's three Russians and a Belorussian. The Russians have been working on the LLM AI for Yandex, the Russian search engine in Runet (the Russian Internet network), and are currently working on the Belorussian version, Tut in the Belnet Three men and a woman. They are in Belorussia working now".

"Get Suzanne down here now, on the double!"

6: Warsaw

"This isn't a Board Meeting, and it isn't even a regular Reaper Project meeting. This is our own little private gathering to discuss matters, let's say, that other people don't have to know about yet… and I want it kept that way. We have *Talent,* what we used to call Human Resources (I never did care much for that term); we have I.T., or Information Technology Infrastructure, as it's called nowadays; R&D, and lil' old me. Melanie, Suzanne, John and Jim. Cosy, eh?

"So, I'll just go over the state of play so that everyone is up to speed. We have been secretly liaising with a small group of East European I.T. specialists. They, or their spokesman, let's get it right, claims that they put together the LLM AI for Yandex, and that they are currently working on the same kind of project in Belarus.

"However, they don't want to live in Belarus or Russia; they want to live over here, or in Europe. I'm not really sure where, and it doesn't matter much for our purposes anyway. The point is, they can't work for us, and the Russians or Belorussians at the same time.

"I propose that our need is the greater, so we should have them!" The other three shared the joke. "So, how are we going to make that happen? A rhetorical question for now. You will all get the chance to have your say later. If you don't know where Belarus is, look at the map I gave you in the hand out. It lies to the north of The Ukraine between Russia and Poland. Why doesn't anyone say *The* Ukraine any more? Never mind. When I was in school, it was *The* Ukraine. No matter. No matter, it's still *The* Ukraine to me. So, there it sits between Russia and Poland, which is in the EU, let me remind you.

"So, they are not that far from freedom technically speaking. In fact, from Minsk to Warsaw, the two capitals is only 350 miles. Ten hours by road, seventy-five minutes by air. That measly distance and a few armed border guards on both sides are all that's keeping us from them… or visa-versa.

"I've got a bit of a frog in my throat this morning, so I'll ask John to take over. John, please".

"Yes, sir. As you know, we have offices in Warsaw, and we have delivery depots scattered throughout the countryside. It is highly likely that admin and distribution in Poland could be better organised or modernised. So, if we were to organise a conference with that goal at our Warsaw headquarters, we could invite these guys over to talk on their master subject – AI. This would be the reason they need to apply to Poland for a Schengen visa to visit Poland. Once there, they have ninety days.

"We could get a lot of groundwork done in ninety days, and assess their ability to head up Reaper for us. If they are not up to scratch, we dump them, if they are we offer them jobs in Europe or the US. They apply for asylum and keep working for us".

"Thank you, but let's stop there for a moment, John. Any questions so far?"

"What if the Russians won't let them leave, or the Polish won't give them a visa? It's not that easy for key Russian personnel to travel to the West at the moment".

"Good point. There are other ways, let's say less usual ways of travelling from country to country, but I don't think that we ought to dwell on that too much at this stage. For now, let's just assume that they get to the conference, and know their onions. John?"

"Given the state of US – Russian relations, it is quite likely that their request for asylum would be granted even if just to upset the Russians. Our intelligence services would probably want to debrief them, which might disrupt our plans, but hopefully by then our path to a fully functioning AI service would be clear enough for our in-house team to carry on unsupervised. Melanie, this is your department".

"Er, yes. We have a very intelligent, well-educated staff-pool, and they are well equipped. If they were given enough pointers and leads, I am confident that they, we, would be able to add the finishing touches to any project".

"Great! That's just what I wanted to hear", said Jim. "So, that just leaves the conference. I'll leave you three to organise that. As I said, just make it look like a normal conference about upgrading our systems out there. You'll all need visas for Poland too. What? I see surprised faces. You three have to be there too. This is your show, so you have to get it on the road. Who else?

"Suzanne, you'll have to find out how to get invitations to your Gang of Four. You'll need to set a date too… try for a fortnight's time, but that might be rushing it a bit. As soon as you can, anyway. I'm anxious to get moving on this.

"Any other questions? OK, that's all for now. John, could I see you in my office?"

The two men passed through the connecting door and sat at Jim's desk. "Well done, John! You've got your team motivated and productive. Have a drink, I'm having one. I think we've deserved it. I won't be going to Warsaw, with you. Cheers! I don't want to leave Marion alone, and she's not up to flying at the moment.

"Nevertheless, I have full confidence in you, and I am only a phone call away. Whether you need me or not, if you get my drift. Keep me in the loop. I don't want to have to phone you to find out what's going on. Phoning in too often is better than phoning in too seldom in this case".

∞

"There's the call to board our San Francisco International Airport flight for London Heathrow. We're on our way ladies!" said John.

"I'm not looking forward to this at all", said Melanie. "It'll be about fifteen hours before we get to Warsaw's Chopin Airport. Fifteen hours! Sheesh!"

"Fifteen hours at $333 an hour just for the cost of one flight, so a grand an hour for the three of us just to get there!" said Suzanne. "Or are they returns? Returns? OK, half that, but it's still quite a lot".

"Why don't you want to go, Mel?" asked Suzanne when they were settled into their seats in Business Class.

"Piotrowski. My married name is Marshall, but my maiden name is Peters, and that is because my grandfather changed it from Piotrowski when he arrived in America after being liberated from a Nazi camp after World War Two. I just don't fancy it. I've never been there and don't want to see it. I'm American, God damn it!... and fifteen hours of travelling!"

"You'll be all right, Mel. We'll have a bottle of champagne... the time will soon pass", said Suzanne, "then it's just a short taxi ride to our hotel, the Raffles Europejski Warsaw. It's only six miles from the airport and we've got the Presidential Suite. Jim has really pushed the boat out for us".

Melanie smiled, but it wasn't a real one. She had taken two tranquillisers and planned on sleeping for the whole flight.

∞

"This place is fantastic!" said John gazing around the room. $3,000 a night, but it's got everything and then some. Do you approve, ladies? We'll draw straws for bedrooms. What's the time diff between here and home. Oh, I haven't put my watch forward yet... it's... Wow! We left San Francisco at 10am on September 15th, and now it's just after 10am on September 16th!"

"We've lost a day of our lives..." said Melanie.

"Well, you chose to sleep through most of it. I thoroughly enjoyed the flight", said John.

"You didn't stop eating, drinking and chatting up the stewardesses..." said Suzanne.

"I was not chatting them up. I was just passing the time of day. Anyway, I'd better phone Jim, and tell him that the Eagle has landed. Can you contact the Russians, Su? See how they're doing and where they are. If they are in Warsaw maybe we could meet them this afternoon, or for dinner – an early dinner".

"I will do that, but first I'm going to have a shower and get changed. There are three bedrooms… One, Two and Three", she said pointing. Then she took a slip of paper off the writing desk, tore it into three pieces and put a number on each. She screwed them up and offered them around. She was left with number two, the master bedroom.

"Well, lucky ol' me. I'll go for my shower then".

Melanie went to her room too, and John sat oh the couch to phone his boss. "Jim? Hi, can you take my call? Great! No, no problem… We've arrived… Yes, minutes ago… It's 10:20 am here… Yes, we are exactly eight hours ahead… Oh, I see. Sorry, Sir. That makes it 02:20 in Palo Alto… Yes, sorry, I didn't mean to wake you up. It took us 24 hours to get here, so I thought it was 10:20 am over there but a day earlier. How stupid of me.

"Anyway, everything is fine. Lovely flight and hotel, and Suzanne is about to make contact with the Russians. What time shall I call you back? In seven hours' time. Certainly, and sorry again".

He looked at Melanie, who was giggling at him from the doorway to her room. "You just woke up the boss at 2am to tell him that you have had a good flight and that the hotel is fantastic! I bet that went down well".

"He was better about it than I would have been. Time for a shower and change of clothing for me too. See you later".

∞

"Oh, John" How funny. Your ears must have been burning after that. I bet Jim was cursing you for waking him up to tell him that you had had a good flight" said Suzanne.

"He was very nice about it, actually, but probably only because Marion was there – probably asleep. When do we get to meet your Russians again?"

"They should be here by two. That's what Ivan said".

"Ivan! I bet that's not his real name. Nobody's actually called Ivan the Russian!"

"Well, it's almost two now, and we are in the bar where we said we'd rendezvous, so all we can do is wait, and have a drink. She pushed the silent buzzer on the table, and a waitress appeared.

Melanie looked at her colleagues. "Mineral water with gas and ice for me, please".j

"A bottle of the local beer for me, please" said John.

"I'll try the beer too", said Suzanne.

"We have traditional Polish beers such as Żywiec, and Okocim or we have local craft beers like Pinta, Kormoran, and AleBrowar".

John looked at Suzanne, who shrugged her shoulders almost imperceptibly. "Two Pintas, please". The waitress, did a short curtsey and left.

"Five past. I hope they're good time-keepers".

"It's not as if we're standing out in the rain, is it, John?" said Suzanne.

"And we don't know where they're coming from, or what hassles they might have. Just enjoy your beer", said Melanie.

John took out his paper notepad and reread the questions he wanted answers to for the umpteenth time.

"They're an hour late already. Does anybody fancy a game of hangman?"

The ladies nodded. "I haven't played that since I was a kid", said Melanie. "I could murder a couple of sandwiches too!"

"Good idea", said John, pushing the buzzer.

"A plate of mixed sandwiches, please. Ham, cheese, salad… that sort of thing, and another round of drinks".

"Not for me", said Suzanne.

The waitress left and John turned the page over on his pad. "OK, no foreign words, and the item has to be connected in some way to this room or what we can see out of the windows. Two words nine and six". The waitress appeared with their order and a bottle of Moskovskaya Vodka.

"We didn't order any vodka", said Melanie.

"No, madame. The party at the far end of the room sent it over with their compliments".

The three turned to look at the table, but they couldn't make anyone out at that distance. Suzanne wrote something on a page from John's notepad, folded it in half and put it on the waitress's tray. "Please give my note to the party that sent us the vodka".

7: Dr. Ivan Ivanovich Petrov

A man approached their table. "Good afternoon. You are Americans, I think, and are waiting for someone? We wanted to make you aware that the party you await has arrived, but we needed to observe you first. I am sure that you understand that not everyone is who they appear to be".

"Would you like to join us, Mister…?"

"Ivan. Yes, I will take the weight off my legs, as you say". He sat on one of the three remaining seats at the table, and smiled at everyone there present. "Do you require anything from me? Which of you beautiful young ladies is Suzie?"

Suzanne blushed, but said that she was. John tried to hide a smile, but Suzanne noticed it and was not impressed. "Are the people you are sitting with over there the other members of your team, Ivan?" asked John.

"The others over there are my immediate family. The other members of the team can be called whenever necessary". Ivan reached over and pushed the button. "Four vodka glasses, a pint of Pinta beer and a bowl of sea salt, please, mademoiselle". The waitress blushed, curtseyed smiling at Ivan, and left. He has a way with women, thought John.

"So, Ivan", asked John, "did you have a pleasant flight from Minsk?"

"Erm, we didn't fly. We arrived by car… or by cars, to be more accurate. Excuse me for appearing to be rude, but could I see some ID, please? Passports, preferably". The three looked at each other quizzically, but handed them over all the same. The waitress delivered the shot glasses and a small bow of sea salt, then left. "Erm, John, please pour the vodka". Ivan continued to scrutinise the passports in his hands and the faces of the people seated at the table.

Then he handed them back, thanked each person and held up his glass, "Za zdorovye". The other three followed his lead.

"Right, Ivan, if that is your real name. We need some bona fides from you now".

"Most certainly", he said handing over his Russian passport. In it, he was identified as Ivan Ivanovich Petrov". John studied the details and photo, although he was by no means an expert, and passed it to his colleagues to do likewise. Meanwhile, Ivan held his profile steady, and poured more shots of vodka.

"Are you satisfied?" he asked.

"It doesn't say Doctor in your passport. Just plain old mister". Nevertheless, John nodded and handed Ivan's passport back to him. "Thank you. Now, I will be totally honest with you in order to prove my good intentions. My name is not Ivan Ivanovich Petrov, and my passport is a fake. You look shocked!

"The government would never have allowed someone like me, or my team, to leave Russian territory. True, they sent us to Minsk, but they consider that within their sphere of influence... Erm, like you Americans do Mexico and Canada. What is more, the EU might not have granted us a visa either because of our professions. They would probably – say, 60% probability – have classified us as potential spies, and refused us visas. So, we, my family and I, and my team, had fake passports made six months ago, and we drove over the Belarus/Polish border where there was no security! Does that shock you too? Well, that is only because you Americans have no idea what life is like here". He poured himself another drink put salt on the edge of his beer glass in the old Russian style, took a large swig of it, and knocked the vodka chaser back. "Za zdorovye!" be said with a big grin.

"Where are you staying, 'Ivan'?" asked John.

"Erm, nearby... in our car. We are hoping that you will put us up somewhere. This hotel seems very nice, and we would be easily accessible to one another".

"Yes, OK, but I have to confirm expenses with my boss. It isn't my money. I can put you up for one night, then I'll talk to my boss and see what he says".

"Very well. Please arrange that now, so my family can bathe and rest et cetera". John looked at Melanie.

"Could you arrange that for Ivan, please, Mel? Ivan, Melanie will need your passport, and your families' too". Ivan took out a mobile phone, spoke into it in Russian, waved, and said, "They will follow you anywhere now. My wife, Sonya, speaks English very well".

He poured himself another vodka and pushed the button to order another beer.

"Why don't you go with Mel, Su? Ivan and I will sit here until you get Ivan's family settled it". She shot him a mean glance, but John fended it off. "Please, it won't take you long, and, you know, cultures are different. Ivan's family won't want me there. I'm sure they would prefer the women's touch". Ivan could see what was happening, and intervened to support John.

"I know that my wife and young children would prefer to meet female strangers than male ones. Male strangers could be secret police, you know?" Everybody knew that female strangers could just as easily be secret police, but no-one said anything. Ivan shrugged at John in recognition of the weakness of his proposition.

When they were alone, Ivan said, "I am hot. The Belarus government will miss me, my family and my team within a few days. I used your company's invitation to the Warsaw conference as a smokescreen, knowing that my visa application would be refused. My suggestion to you now, is to cancel the conference. Say something like your CEO has been taken ill with Covid-19 and can't attend.

"I told my boss in Minsk that my family were homesick, so I was going to take them on a five-day holiday into The Minsk Uplands. Mobile phone coverage is very patchy up there. I also gave all my staff five days off too. That means that we have four days before the authorities will come looking for me – us.

"I left my mobile phone on a park bench yesterday, so that could be anywhere by now, and may give us a bit more time, but the SVR, erm, the Russian Foreign Intelligence Service is not stupid. Eventually, they will see through whatever ruse we invent. To be safe, we have three days, if you cancel the conference today". Ivan stared at John, while pouring them both another vodka, and ringing the bell.

"I will need to talk to my boss".

"I'm sure you will, but the clock is ticking. The more chaff we can put up, the more chance we have of putting the SVR off the scent. I still don't know which company you and your fragrant companions represent, but if the CEO wants my help, then, you need to get me, my family and my team out of here quickly. Warsaw is not safe for us, neither is Berlin. Nowhere is, to tell the truth, but we would feel safer if we were a long, long way away from here. Za zdorovye". John clinked glasses, but he realised that he was out of his depth.

"What about seeking asylum at the American Embassy?"

Ivan grimaced and hunched his shoulders. "It is a possible route, but not guaranteed, and would take a long time. We would all need to be interviewed by the CIA, the military, the Embassy staff, lawyers and God knows who else". John just nodded, as if to say, 'Obviously, and?'

"You don't get it, do you, John?"

"This is not my master subject, no…"

Ivan adopted the attitude of a teacher at a remedial school. "If your boss sent you to do this job… if he or she chose someone who doesn't know what they are doing, to do this job, then they don't know what they are doing either. Please, excuse me. I am not trying to be offensive. You are probably very highly qualified in your area of expertise, but I doubt that that involves smuggling Russian émigrés out of a country under the noses of the SVR, does it?"

"No, but we haven't committed to doing that either".

"Forgive me, John, but you just mentioned asylum. I'll tell you what that would probably mean. We are seven people. My family of four, and three others in the team. That is at least two or three days each for our initial assessment and the verification of our backgrounds and stories. Let's call it three weeks.

"If, and that could be a big if, if we are deemed to be of interest and possible use to the USA – note that well, John, use to the USA, not your company – your company will not get a look in – if we are deemed to be of possible use to your government, then the real interviews will begin. Interviews by the Department of State, the CIA, the military, lawyers, embassy staff. And, all that data will have to be checked, cross-referenced, verified and assessed for our potential usefulness to the government of the USA, not our usefulness to your company.

"That could easily take a month or two. So, let's say that three months from walking into the embassy to seek asylum, all of our applications are looked upon favourably, then U.S. officials would have to consider the diplomatic ramifications of offering asylum to foreign nationals, especially from a nation like Russia, because it has a strained relationship with the U.S., let's say because of Ukraina. The U.S. may issue temporary or emergency documentation to facilitate our safe departure from Poland to the U.S., always assuming that the asylum claim meets the required standards. If the asylum request is granted, the U.S. Embassy may provide temporary shelter until arrangements can be made to transfer us asylum-seekers to the United States.

"This transfer is typically done discreetly, sometimes with assistance from U.S. law enforcement or intelligence agencies, to avoid attracting undue attention and to ensure the safety of the individuals. This takes time to arrange. There are many Russian spies in Warsaw like in Berlin. Let's say another month for that. Where are we now? Four months…"

"I get the picture, Ivan".

"No, you don't. Let me finish. You need to know all this, because you are going to have to explain it to your boss. So, we have now been smuggled out of Poland and have arrived in the good old U.S. of A. and asylum processing begins in earnest, which would involve further interviews with U.S. Citizenship and Immigration Services (the USCIS) and potentially the FBI or / *and* the CIA, if they think that we might hold classified information, which we do.

"During this period, which could easily take two or three months, we will be housed on some military complex and kept away from civilians, which includes you and your boss, I should imagine". Ivan raised his eyebrows and John nodded.

"So, that is six months, if everything goes well. Six months of isolation from your company and its AI aspirations. One last detail, by then, we will hold American passports, and won't feel indebted to your firm for helping us, because you won't have, and we will be at liberty to seek better jobs from your competitors.

"I think that you will find that that's a reasonable, fair and comprehensive assessment of your predicament, John, but you talk it over with your boss. Don't take too long over it though, because we can still just walk into that embassy and take our chances anyway – without you". He poured two more vodkas, rang the buzzer again and put on an innocent face.

John had decided that he liked the man. Ivan was clearly intelligent, and knew his own worth. He was also caring – he had brought his family with him, and loyal, because he was looking out for his team. He had included them in all his explanations so far. He flipped up the page of his notepad, and looked at his questions, most of which seemed childishly irrelevant at that moment.

"One thing, Ivan. Well, one thing in particular. Suzanne has spoken to you about our plans to have an LLM AI system in place, how long do you think it would take to get one up and running? Just a rough idea, so I have something to tell my boss. He's sure to ask".

"How many shots of vodka does it take to make someone fall over? Or as you say, how long is a piece of string? What do you want to use it for? How many access points will it have? How many users at one time? What is the range of the AI's database? What sort of controls do you want to put on its answers? What can its answers not divulge? What level of censorship does your company and the government require?"

"Yes, I get your point. Does 'average' sound a bit stupid?"

Ivan pursed his lips. "Not for a layman, I suppose. We have the basic structure already. We would need to find solutions to the questions I just posited, and a few hundred more, but we could have a rambling, fairly stupid giant of an AI model up and stumbling about – not quite running, you understand – in four to six weeks, but it would need a lot of training.

"This is usually done at the expense of a limited section of the I.T.-savvy public, which has proved to be fascinated by AI, and has, is happily putting up with all AI's teething problems, which is providing us with the training our models need. How far have you got with your project – what's it called?"

"Er, Reaper".

"How far have you got with Reaper?"

"We have christened it Reaper"

"That's all? You have only given it a name? I see… You do need help. Still no matter, we can fix something up for you".

When do we get to meet the rest of the team?

"Um, you talk to your boss first. When can you do that?"

John looked at his watch. It was six fifteen, so he was an hour and a quarter late for phoning Jim. "I'll do it right away".

"OK. I'll go and see my family and be back at seven thirty. Is that all right with you?".

"Sure. See you at seven-thirty".

8: Reality Kicks In

"I'm sorry I missed your nine o'clock call, sir. Things are moving so fast here, and I think I'm still jet-lagged".

"First you wake me up at two-thirty a.m. to tell me you had a lovely flight, and then you keep me waiting for an hour and a half because you're tired and busy! It's not good enough, John. Do you want me to put one of the others in charge?"

"No, sir. I'll buck up. I'll get to grips with it. We met Ivan late this evening – that's how I came to miss our call. I was talking to him. The plan we had is going to have to be completely re-written. First off, Ivan is not his real name, but he and his family do have passports – fake passports – that look real. Well, are real, according to Ivan, but are illegal. Anyway, they should fool anyone who doesn't check with government records.

"I mentioned asylum to him, but he reckons that that would mean about six months of U.S. government and CIA processing during which he would be incommunicado… Yes, sir, six months!

"No, that is no good to us. He can't just stay here and work at our Warsaw office either because he crossed the

Belarus border illegally. There is no immigration stamp into Poland in his passport. If he tried to work, he would be deported and almost certainly imprisoned.

"Yes, sir, I agree. It is a mess. However, not only that, but he is now on the run from the Russian CIA, the RSV, I think he said. He took five days leave from work, so if he doesn't go back in, they will be looking for him and his colleagues in three days' time. No, I haven't met them yet. Maybe this evening at seven-thirty. Eleven-thirty your time. He's a shrewd customer. I think he's holding the team back until he hears what you have to say.

"Well, yes. I do like him, actually, but he's very careful. Cunning and shrewd, I'd say, but also loyal and charming. He says that he has his LLM AI project hidden in the cloud, and that he can have a working prototype operational within two months, but obviously not if he is being handled by U.S Immigration. Yes, sir. My tendency is to believe him. He's either Russia's answer to Lawrence Olivier, or he knows what he's talking about.

"Oh, one last thing. They all slept in their cars last night. I have put Ivan and his family in a family room, should I give the other three rooms too? OK, will do".

"OK, sir I'll await your call… at about eight-thirty to nine o'clock. Yes, sir… No, sir. Bye for now, sir".

"Mel, you know the procedure for booking rooms, could you take care of that, please?"

"You look hen-pecked", said Melanie.

"I feel like it too, and brow-beaten. Anyway, a quick shower and then down to meet Ivan".

∞

When John's phone rang at eight-thirty, he answered it and moved away from Ivan and his colleagues to sit at an empty table some yards away.

"Are you able to talk confidentially, John? Good. I don't like having this conversation on the phone. Not even these hi-tech super-duper encrypted satellite things we're using. Listen carefully and make scant notes if you have to. Tonight, tell the receptionist that your party, including the Russians, are going sightseeing tomorrow morning, and that you want a nine o'clock call. Ask her to have packed meals delivered to your rooms in hampers. Also tell her that you have a taxi booked for eleven am, and that they should call you when it arrives.

"Eat the food, or flush it down the toilet. Pack what clothes you want to take with you in the hampers. Get ten backpacks too. Fill them with clothes. Everything else, you're going to have to leave behind. Count them as lost forever, unless we can get them forwarded. That might be possible.

"The taxi-driver will be a black guy with a Caribbean accent. Let anybody who's listening in find one of those at short notice, eh, John? Anyway, he will hand you a piece of paper with the word 'Bombardier' on it and my signature. It'll be a photocopy, so don't expect a wet one. Then follow this guy, all of you, the Russians too. They'll lose most of their stuff too, unless we can get it forwarded

"I don't want to say any more. Just do everything that the Caribbean guy tells you to – as it were me in person".

"So, all ten of us?"

"Yes, all ten of you".

The phone went dead, but John sat there for a moment making notes, and wondering what the Hell Jim had in mind for them the next day. When he rejoined the others, his colleagues looked at him expectantly, but he just said 'Later' and sat down.

When he did judge it safe to talk, John told the other three what he had been told, Ivan stood up to leave.

"Where are you going?" asked John.

"First, I am going to tell the others, and then I'm going to sell my car. It shouldn't take more than an hour. I'll see you back here with the others".

"Why is it that I get the impression that Ivan knows more than we do?" asked John.

∞

When Ivan returned an hour later, he was flanked by three younger people, two men and a woman. Ivan was head and shoulders taller than all of them. He looked to be in his mid-forties, the man to his left in his mid-thirties, and the boy and girl holding hands to his right in their mid-twenties.

"I think it would be safe to cancel one of the rooms", said Melanie.

"I would like to introduce you to our team", said Ivan. "This is Eduard". Eduard held out his hand to the three Americans; and the love-birds are Alex and Katya. They blushed and nodded, but didn't offer to shake hands. Covid had made it less likely for younger people to shake hands in many countries.

"Sit down. Join us. What can we get you?" asked Suzanne. "Something hot or sandwiches, salad, you name it". She handed them the menu when they were seated. "Did you manage to sell your vehicles? Why did you do that? Security? Were they known to the Russian Security Forces?"

"Erm, they do understand English, because it is the language of programming and coding, but they have never had much opportunity to speak it, especially with native speakers. It will take them a little while to get used to it… and your accents. Yes, we sold our cars, because we won't be needing them any more, but didn't get the full market value. That's all right though, at least we got something".

Ivan hadn't quite answered Suzanne's questions, but she didn't want to labour the point so let it drop. When they had eaten a meal and socialised a little. John suggested that they go to their suite to 'discuss affairs', by which he meant arrangements for the following day.

"I don't like to contradict you in public, John, but I think that it is safer to talk business right where we are", said Ivan.

"But we don't want to be overheard" replied John.

"Exactly so", said Ivan. "I have an app on my phone, which I wrote myself, and it scans the local vicinity for listening devices – bugs, as you say. It is highly accurate to about two point three metres in all directions. So, I estimate, that if we keep our voices to a normal level, given the amount of background noise, which is 67 decibels, according to another app that I wrote, we cannot be overheard after about two metres. Unless someone approaches our table. However, people from countries like ours are all self-taught to watch their surroundings for intruders and eavesdroppers, which is why Russians don't look at the face of the person they are talking to". Ivan could see the blank stares from the Americans.

"A Russian wouldn't tell a stranger, or someone he didn't trust, anything that could incriminate him, so he doesn't need to worry about anyone overhearing. That is when he will try to read your face! On the other hand, if he trusts you, and is passing on secrets, he will be trusting you and so doesn't have to study your face, so he will be looking for eavesdroppers – that's what you call them, isn't it?"

"Eh, yes", said Melanie checking with her colleagues.

"So, we know that we are safe here, but the same cannot be said for your suite, can it? This is the best hotel in Warsaw.

Many important, even very important people stay here. Russia is sure to have an agent working on the hotel staff. Probably a cleaner, or a repairman, so that they can bug the rooms – and suites – of rich and famous foreigners". He was smiling.

"Well, I'll be jiggered!" said John. "The thought hadn't crossed my mind that we could be bugged…"

"No. You're not Russian, nor are you in an intelligent service – sorry, I mean 'intelligence service' – of course". He smiled again. John suspected that the slip was intentional, but he let it go.

"Well, thank you, Ivan, for my first lesson in counter-espionage", said John.

"Ivan is good teacher, no?" said the young Belarusian woman in the team. It was the first thing that John could remember her saying since they met.

John smiled back at her fresh, innocent-looking face, "Yes, very good".

Ivan smiled, nodded in acceptance of the compliment and sipped his beer. "So, John, what have you got to tell us about tomorrow?"

"Before, I get into that, does anyone want anything from the bar?"

"May I handle this, John?"

"Yes, by all means. Mel could you go to the hotel shop in the lobby, please? I noticed that they sell backpacks, but I forgot to look when they close. He revealed his watch".

"Sure, Do, you want to help me carry ten rucksacks, Su?"

"Staff will deliver them to our rooms", said Ivan nonchalantly, guessing that ten meant one each. "So, we are going on a trip tomorrow. I like rambling", he said pushing the buzzer.

When the waitress appeared, Ivan ordered. "Another round of drinks, please. Two pints of beer for myself and a bottle of Moskovskaya. Then for hors d'oeuvre, some dried fish – Russian style… do you have 'vobla'? Excellent! And some Polish kabanosy, and assorted pickles, dried cheese, and variety of nuts …

"Add in whatever types of smoked sausages, marinated mushrooms, and salted herring you may have, and make it enough for fifteen people. We are all very appreciative of Polish cooking!" He smiled broadly at the young waitress, and spread his arms to indicate all the people at the table.

When the ladies returned from their mini shopping expedition, Melanie said, "The bags have been sent up to our rooms… Who ordered all that? I haven't seen Polish food like that since my grandmother died!" Tears were forming in her eyes.

"I did", said Ivan. Are you of Polish extraction, Melanie? Then this is a banquet for you. I bet it's not like Americanised Polish food. This is the real McCoy".

Melanie looked at him, but was busy dabbing her eyes.

When John had finished explaining what he knew about the plans for the following day, there was a silence of about fifteen seconds, before Ivan broke it, and said, "It looks like this is our last night in Eastern Europe then".

"We don't know that, Ivan. You haven't even got proper credentials…"

"Maybe not, but that didn't stop us getting this far. I think that tomorrow we will be in the West, the real West – probably Germany – and if we take that step, it would be very unwise, stupid even, to ever return to Eastern Europe again – even Poland, because the Russians can pick people up here and spirit them out of the country more easily that a child can steal candy from a sweetshop".

Katya giggled, but put her hand over her mouth when she saw the Americans looking at her. Alex gave her a playful nudge with his elbow.

"So, my friends, enjoy your authentic Russian vobla, and Polish snacks, because it will be the last time we will get the chance".

At ten-thirty, when John suggested that it might be a good idea to turn in, most people got up, but Ivan said, "You go ahead, my friends, however, I am feeling homesick for Mother Russia and the East all ready. I am going to sit here until they throw me out, or midnight, or one a.m. at least. That still gives me eight hours' sleep, and if my intuition is correct, we will have plenty of time to sleep tomorrow. We aren't going to be burning much physical energy… Emotional, and psychological energy? Yes, I think so, but I predict that we will spend most of tomorrow seated in a vehicle".

"I'll stay for an hour or so too, Ivan, if I won't be intruding on your melancholy", said Melanie. "I am American, but Polish by blood. I've never thought about it much, but being here now for the first time, seeing this food again, and the background music… plus the fact that I will never see it again… Well, I want to make the most of our last few hours, just in case Ivan is right".

"In that case, I'll stay too", said John sitting back down. "Good night, see you tomorrow!" he said to the others, and turned his attention back to the bar snacks. "These are absolutely delicious!" he said.

9: Exodus

"Mr. Dickenson, sir. There is a gentleman at reception claiming that you booked a ride from him yesterday. May I say something, sir? Something doesn't seem right. He's, erm, a black man, who doesn't speak Polish. It is odd, no? I can't remember the last time I saw a black man working in Warsaw, and how can it be... a taxi driver who doesn't speak Polish? Most Polish people don't speak English... and he has a strange accent... a bit like reggae. Shall I contact security?"

"No, no Heaven forbid! That sounds exactly like the man I booked a sightseeing trip with yesterday. He works for a firm that uses him on special occasions like showing English-speaking tourists around.

"Don't do anything. We'll be down immediately".

"Come on, ladies, time is of the essence! Down to reception on the double. Can you manage that hamper between you? I have to alert Ivan".

The three left the suite together with John on the phone. "Ivan, it's showtime, our taxi driver is in reception, and they are getting suspicious. Please get your family and team downstairs to the lobby immediately".

While Melanie and Suzanne went to sit in the lobby, John went up to reception. There was no mistaking his driver.

"Hi, do you have anything for me?" he asked as he drew the driver away from the suspicious receptionist, who, he assumed, was trying to listen in.

"Yes, I do that", he replied smiling and handed him a folded note. It read 'Bombardier' and was sighed in Jim's distinctive, flamboyant manner.

"Great! I'm John, and your name?"

"You can call me, Richard", but he pronounced it REE-chard.

John didn't know whether to call him Richard, as in standard English or as he had pronounced it. "We're just waiting for the others. Ah, here they come now. Where are you parked?"

"I parked the minibus right outside, man. Get the staff to carry your things outside that door there, and I'll go get the bus", as he walked off, John remembered Jim's instructions: *'Just do everything that the Caribbean guy tells you to — as it were me in person'*. Come on, Ivan, our transport is here". He looked at Melanie and Suzanne and pointed at the door. Bellboys immediately relieved the visitors of their luggage hoping for tips.

Richard parked the Mercedes-Benz Sprinter less than three metres outside the entrance, and everyone piled into the luxury vehicle. "Not a bad jalopy, eh, man?" said Richard grinning into the rear-view mirror.

"Not bad at all", agreed John, who hadn't been in a bus since his college days at Harvard. "Where did you get this?"

"I hired it. It's the sleekest bus I've ever driven. The only bus I've ever driven too, so that's not saying much is it?" he laughed. John gulped, and didn't feel like laughing.

"Can you handle a big vehicle like this, Richard? I mean, are we safe enough?"

"We're safe enough in here, you know, but I can't rightly say the same for those people out there who get too close to us!" and he laughed again.

"Can you tell us where you are taking us, please", asked Melanie.

"Well, madam, I would if I could, but I don't read Polish, and have trouble remembering and pronouncing the names that I have been told, so I am just following the satnav. I'm used to satnav, I use that every day".

"Thank God for that", said John under his breath. "Does satnav tell you how long it'll take us to get there?"

"That's a fine question! I can answer you that one for sure. Assuming good weather, light traffic, no police check points, and no mechanical failure, ETA is one hour and forty-three minutes from now. We are taking the scenic route west-southwest. However, we might need to stop off to waste time, depending on alterations to the plan". That was in the direction of where Poland adjoined Germany and Czechia. Ivan was grinning from ear to ear.

"If you want something to eat, there are some things in the fridge, but we can stop somewhere for lunch, if you like. We have a lot of time".

"Is there any beer in the fridge?" asked Ivan.

"No, I don't think so, but we can stop in the first village when we get out of Warsaw. According to the print-out I got this morning, we will take the Trakt Królewski route, and the first notable village we're likely to encounter is *Pęcice,* which is located about 15 km from central Warsaw. Then it mentions Nadarzyn, Żabia Wola, and Mszczonów, but I don't have any details on the villages themselves. We should be in Pęcice within twenty to thirty minutes".

'Please awake me when we arrive in Pęcice". Katya looked at Ivan and smiled as he closed his eyes – he was a hero to her. They stopped several times to pick up supplies or use the facilities along the way, and had lunch in a village pub that they noticed. It was a very pleasant journey. Melanie was particularly interested in observing the villages and the farmers working the land, because that was where her family would have been – in a field - before the war. She wasn't sure where, exactly, but that hardly mattered.

While everyone else was either dozing or staring out of the window, John was talking to Richard.

"We've made good time", said Richard. "A little too good actually. Do you think that your party would appreciate stretching their legs in another village?"

"I'm sure they wouldn't mind at all, but it's irrelevant really. We are in your hands. If they don't want to get out, they can stay in the bus. It's your call, Richard!"

"OK, a few hours in *Rzgów* it is. There should be a pub and church to explore and possibly a couple of local shops. Last chance to get authentic Polish country-style food".

Ivan and Eduard chose to go to the pub, which had been predictable, and everyone else was expected to rendezvous there in two hours' time, because the minibus was parked outside it. That would give everybody an hour in the pub to calm down before the next stage in their journey.

"What are you going to do, Richard?"

"Why, John, man, I'm going to act like a cab driver – put my feet up and have a kip in the cab". John smiled.

"OK, are you coming into the pub at five?"

"For sure! I'll be there, and if not, I'll be here, and you can wake me up".

At five fifty-five, John paid the bar bill, and asked, "What now, Richard?"

"Now my friends, comes the next stage, but first we have to get back into the bus". Once there, he continued, "Please take the batteries out of your phones. You must be completely incommunicado until I give you the all clear. Please take out your phones' batteries and place them in the bag I am giving you. John, could you collect up the bags, please?

"Thank, you. Now we can proceed". He started the vehicle and pointed it onto the road out. It was beginning to get dark, and some people thought they knew what was going on. Fifteen minutes later, Richard pulled over. Ivan, I need you now.

"Right ', said Richard turning around at the wheel, "This is a tricky bit. Not three metres over that bush, is a wire fence. We have already cut it for you. We have also shot out at least one of the perimeter lights. It will be getting dark in ten minutes, so, we need to work quickly. I will take the Americans to immigration, but you others have to get to the sky-blue jet. You won't be able to miss it. It is quite a size. There are probably movement sensors attached to lights, so keep under cover. Here are three powerful air pistols. If a light comes on, put it out of action. However, no matter what happens, don't shoot at anyone. They will all have bigger guns than we do".

Turning to the American women, he said, "One of you has to pretend to be sick at emigration. It might buy us some time… say that your medication is on the plane. Say that we brought it to you because you suspected a medical emergency … you had a gut feeling… That sort of thing. Pretend to panic.

"Ivan, get as close to the jet as you dare. If someone opens the door at the top of the staircase, run for it and get inside. Likewise, if you see us coming from emigration try to board the plane seconds before we do. Good luck, everyone.

We should be all right, so don't worry, but keep together and keep quiet. We'll meet up on the plane". He hi-fived them as they left the minibus and lay in the grass. Then he gave a quiet beep on the horn, and took to the road.

When they turned into the car park, Richard let his passengers out at the VIP entrance and took the bus around to the back of the administration block. He parked it between the plane and the perimeter fence by the staircase as if he had luggage to onboard. I also provided some cover to the others. It was dark by then.

Suddenly, the doors of the VIP exit to the tarmac flew open as did the planes entrance door. Two cabin staff hurried to help their 'stricken' passenger, and Ivan propelled his family and colleagues up the steps keeping low . The jet's engines powered up as John and the American women were assisted up the air stairs.

Minutes later, the aircraft was taxiing down the runway, and 5,500 metres later they were airborne.

"That went better than we ever had the right to hope for", said Richard. "Excuse me, a few minutes. The cabin crew will look after you in the meantime ".

When Richard returned he was dressed in the uniform of a pilot, but had his cap in his hand. Everyone was surprised. Eduard reacted the most. His mouth dropped open and stayed on his chest, until Ivan nudged him and said, "In the West, it is normal to put your hand over your mouth when you yawn ".

"I must apologise for my colleague. There are very, very few black people in Russia, and they are not encouraged to succeed. Congratulations, Richard, you have done a remarkable job to get us out of the East. We are certainly flying over a western country by now, but what is our final destination, if you don't mind my asking?"

"No, no problem, but no-one knows. I certainly don't anyway, but we are flying in the direction of Canada. We have plenty of fuel for a non-stop flight, but Canada is large, as you all know. Our ETA for a landing site in central Canada , say Winnipeg, is four a.m.

"We have a galley on board and a well-stocked bar, so please avail yourselves of the facilities. The cabin staff are on hand to assist. Now, if you will excuse me, I have duties to attend to on the flight deck".

After they had dined and had a glass of wine, John thought that it was probably a good time to update his boss, but he had no idea what time is was in Silicon valley, because he didn't know where they were. He pushed the buzzer for assistance, and a stewardess appeared.

"Excuse me but, could you tell me where the aircraft is, I need to know the time in Silicon Valley so I can phone my boss".

"I'm afraid not, sir", she said firmly. The charterer of this flight has left strict instructions that there should be no communication between us and them".

"I don't think you understand. Could I speak to Flight Officer Richard, please?"

"I'm afraid not, sir. The captain is resting until he takes over the flight deck. However, it was on his clear instructions that there should be no external communication from this aircraft. I apologise for the inconvenience, sir, but we have to comply with the wishes of the party that hires the aircraft, not its passengers. Can I assist you with anything else, sir?"

He wanted to say that she hadn't assisted him with anything yet, but he knew that it wasn't her fault. "Just another cold beer, please, mademoiselle", he said imitating Ivan's way with women. She smiled, but he didn't receive the same kind of smile that Ivan usually got.

The American contingent of the flight had been on private jets before, but the Russians and the Belarusian had not. As John drifted off to sleep, he tried to ignore the row coming from them. He hadn't yet realised that they were not only celebrating being on a luxurious aircraft. The main reason for their exuberance was the prospect of a new life in the West.

The celebrations were still on-going when a member of the cabin crew advised the passengers that they were approaching the destination airport. They buckled in and sobered up realising that they were not home and dry quite yet. In fact, not by a long chalk. When they had landed, the crew of the aircraft lined up to wish them well. "Where are we, Richard?" asked John.

"I am afraid that I am not at liberty to divulge that information, John. The charterer has left strict instructions on what we may tell you. I can tell you though that you are on one of the American continents, and that your onward connection awaits you. Everything has gone well, according to plan.

As John was the last of his party to leave the aircraft, Richard walked down the stairs with him. "Let me accompany you to your next vehicle".

The early morning air was chilly for the Americans, but not for the others. John had an idea that they were in Canada, but didn't say anything. "There she is!" pointed Richard. All fuelled up and ready to depart. This point signifies the end of my mission, John. Please follow your new captain's directions, as carefully as you have mine, and you will soon be home safe and sound in a few hours.

"Ladies and gentlemen, please board the aircraft in front of you via the air stair, and follow the instructions of the captain who is standing at the foot of them". The two captains exchanged perfunctory salutes and smiles.

"A Dornier 228?" asked John.

"Oh, you are acquainted with this aircraft?" asked Richard.

"Yes, they are transporters. Flying haulage".

"They are not as salubrious as a Bombardier Global, that is true, but I am sure that your employer, or the charterer has taken your comfort into account. Well, I have to leave now.

Busy, busy, busy, and I know that the captain there is anxious to leave while it is still dark".

John extended his hand. "Thanks for all you've done for us, Richard". He was the last to board the rather cramped Dornier and took his seat. His American colleagues had expressions of disdain on their faces that John found hilarious, but the Eastern Europeans were still in high spirits.

He closed his eyes as the plane thundered down the runway, so that he didn't have to talk to anyone, and memories of flying in Dorniers years before came flooding back to him. The noise coming from the twin-engine, short take-off and landing turboprop aircraft was uncomfortable. At 90 dB, it was like riding a lawnmower without ear-defenders, which were not being provided to them either. In the days before he became a director at My Media, when he was part of the managerial team at one of My Media' depots, he would sometimes cadge a lift in a Dornier 228 as it was delivering merchandise to other depots in the state.

However, that was long before he had developed a taste for the high-end luxury that he could now afford, and which was so often heaped upon him because of his position in the firm.

His guess was that they were in one of the charter planes that My Media used for distribution, and that they would be hedge-hopping for the next thousand miles… possibly even to his old depot itself.

Three hours later, he was proven right. John recognised his old distribution depot in the Santa Cruz Mountains, in the south of Silicon Valley. It was a secluded, steep terrain, rich in dense forests, yet close enough to tech-centres in Palo Alto and Mountain View. It even had its own private STOL-capable airfield built on the mountain flats with a runway extending about 1,100 metres, which had been purposely designed and build for aircraft like the Dornier 228. Despite being secluded, it was close enough to a highway to integrate road logistics seamlessly.

John's esteem for Jim, or whoever had planned this operation, leapt when they stepped down onto the tarmac. Two people carriers were waiting to take them around to a side entrance to the admin block 50 metres away. Jim wasn't there to welcome them, but the depot manager was. It was his former deputy, Arnold. They greeted each other warmly, before he showed the party up to the top of the building via a lift. "Welcome to your new home", he said as he ushered them into an office, where there was a buffet and a large fridge 50-50 full of drinks and perishable foodstuff.

"Relax, you've made it," said Arnold. "Congratulations!. Help yourselves to whatever we have. We weren't sure what our guests ate and drank, but we got what European food and drink we could find".

"It's fine, Arnold. You've done a grand job. Don't worry about it".

"Thanks, John. I have some instructions to pass on. Mr Diamond says that Melanie and Suzanne can go home, but he stresses that they cannot disclose anything that has happened in the last 36 hours. He says that the cover story is that the conference was cancelled, probably postponed because certain undisclosed 'key personnel' had contracted Covid-19. You three were instantly recalled when you developed gastroenteritis. As far as everyone, friends and family are concerned, you returned by private jet because the commercial airlines were fully booked, but try not to mention it. Our European friends will be accommodated here, or in the next three rooms, which we have partly refurbished for them. John, Mr Diamond has requested that you stay here tonight as well. One of the guest rooms has been prepared for you too. You are in the suite next to mine".

John knew exactly the one he meant. It was reserved for visiting dignitaries, and was basically on the roof, next to the depot manager's suite for when he worked late or stayed over for some reason. Arnold did not live there.

"You may phone your wife to tell her you're back. The Europeans will not be allowed any communication with the outside world.

"If anyone wants to get some sleep, Ivan and his family are next door to the left. The door is marked '1', then Eduard, number two, and our young couple number three. If you need anything, call the switchboard from the telephones in your rooms, but allow a good ten minutes for someone to get to you.

"I'll leave you to it. You must be worn out! Melanie, and Suzanne, if you'll follow me, I will arrange rides home for you. Good night everyone.

"Oh, before I go. Mr Diamond understands what an ordeal you have all had, so tomorrow is a 'free day'. You will not be woken up. You have no meetings or engagements. To our friends. This room will be kept fully stocked, or the fridge will be, at all times. Just help yourselves. We will explain more permanent arrangements when you become available tomorrow".

10: Team Reaper Is Born

John went down to the buffet room of earlier that morning at noon, where he found all of the Europeans, looking decidedly the worse for wear, at lunch. They exchanged greetings. He poured himself a mug of coffee, knowing that he was not at his best either, and took a Danish pastry out of the fridge.

"So, how is everyone?" He glanced around the nodding faces.

"We are all very happy to be here", said Ivan. "Are we permitted to go outside?"

"I don't know, is the truth, but I think it is better not to at the moment. This operation, this company, is in a very secluded location, but there are hundreds of people working here. We don't want to provoke any idle gossip or awkward questions. Not just yet, anyway. Wait for my boss to explain the way forward

"There is a roof garden though. I'll speak to Arnold later, and try to get you permission to use it. Do you have any other questions?"

Ivan's wife, Sonya, said "I don't want to appear ungrateful, but I am concerned about our girls. Natasha and

Alexia are ten and twelve years old. That is a crucial age as far as education goes. I don't want them to miss out. I also think it is inappropriate for them to have to sleep with us". John agreed.

"I was teacher, so I am happy to home-school them, but I will need materials".

"OK", replied John, "well, we are a media company, if we can't provide you with the materials that you need, it doesn't exist in the West. I will talk to Arnold about your girls. I'm sure there is something that can be done. Are the girls computer literate?"

"Of course".

"I see you have your Russian laptops with you. Have you plugged them into the Internet yet?"

"No," said Ivan indignantly. "We are well aware that they could be traceable. I.T. is our game, our professional game, and we are rather good at it, don't you remember?"

"Yes, of course, excuse me. I will have six new computers sent up so you can transfer your data onto them, and get back on line… Cell pones too, I presume?"

"Thank you"

"No problem. I'll get back to you in a few hours. Watch some TV, relax. You're safe now Write down the titles of the books you need, Sonya".

∞

"How has your afternoon been, Ivan?" asked John.

"We don't like being cooped up like this, but we have been transferring the data from our old devices onto the new ones. The old ones should now be destroyed, or sent to Africa by some charity, if you can guarantee that they won't be used in America. It would be a very funny wild goose chase for the SVR to charge over to Rwanda or wherever, when they are first used online, only to find some village kid at school in the jungle. I would love to see that".

John could see that that would be funny, and smiled.

"Did I ever tell you that I was in the KGB, and am a serving officer in the FBS?" He took a slug of his beer, knowing full well that he hadn't. John almost choked on the cake he was eating.

"No, I did not know that, because no, you didn't tell me or any of my team…"

"I was recruited into the KGB, which stands for Komitet Gosudarstvennoy Bezopasnosti, while I was still at university in Moscow. I attended the MITP. Do you know it, or of it? No? The Moscow Institute of Physics and Technology. It is common to be recruited at university. The intelligence services ask most of the most gifted students, and most of them accept, because it opens doors and pays some money, which students always need more of.

"Anyway, when the KGB was dissolved in 1991 after the dissolution of the Soviet Union, its functions were divided into several new agencies. The Federal Security Service, or

FSB or Federalnaya Sluzhba Bezopasnosti in full, took over most of the KGB's domestic security and counter-intelligence functions. I was put in the FSB, and offered a doctorate at the MITP's prestigious Centre for Artificial Intelligence, the CAI.

"When I passed out of there with flying colours, I was made a colonel in the FSB. It doesn't mean anything. It never did, I had no counter-intelligence rôle except that I was supposed to pass on the names of anyone whom I thought was 'a bit dodgy'. I didn't think that anyone was, so never did. I got away with being so unproductive in the FSB, by being so productive in the CAI. It's no big deal".

"No, maybe not, but I will have to tell Mr Diamond, now that I know. It may have some bearing on how the government will treat you when you eventually hand yourself in".

"Yes. I, and my colleagues are fully aware that we cannot escape detection ad infinitum. We will need to plan for that day very carefully".

"Yes, my friend, but let's not worry about it now. You've got your new hardware. I will arrange for your old stuff to be collected. Arnold has said that you can use the roof garden, but that you are not allowed to talk to any of the staff that you might meet there... gardeners, technicians, people like that.

"Tomorrow, we will move Eduard down the corridor, and cut a doorway in the adjoining wall in your room making

Eduard's old room accessible from yours. The girls can move in there… and lastly, go to our website My Media, and find the ISBN's of the media that Sonya wants and we'll get it for you, along with pens, exercise books and all that kind of stuff.

"Well, I have to go again for a chat with the boss – it was scheduled, it is not about you being in the FSB".

"If your CIA is any good, they will already know that many of the intelligentsia that have sensitive jobs, also hold a rank in the FSB. It is a fairly common occurrence in Britain, here and most other countries. It makes sense, no? Why wouldn't such organisations want the best minds around? It is preposterous to think that they would recruit grave-diggers as colonels, isn't it?"

∞

The following morning , John entered their private dining room at eight am, hoping that the Europeans would be there. He was not disappointed. "Good morning! Is everyone fit and raring to go?" he asked.

"We certainly are", said Ivan, "We can't wait to get back to the job we all love and are really good at. Once we have our team set up, you will be amazed at the progress we can make in a relatively short time".

"I'm sure that Mr Diamond will be pleased to hear it. What is the first stage in this process, what equipment will you need, and will you require a particular environment?"

"The first stage in the process is to form a team of specialists. For that, we will need pens and paper, or a printer. Where do you want us to work?"

"Anywhere you are permitted to be…"

"Right here is fine. Next question, please?"

"The next question is, how long will that take?"

"Let's say several hours, and then another hour or two to explain it to someone who is in a position to understand and fulfil our team requirements".

"So, if I brought in the heads of our company's I.T; Recruitment; and Research and Development departments at, say, three pm, you would expect to be ready to talk to them?"

"Yes, John. We will have our list of basic requirements with regard to personnel and equipment by three o'clock this afternoon. The only thing that we need right now is quiet, and writing equipment".

"No problem. The only people with permission to enter this room besides yourselves and the girls, are myself; Melanie; Suzanne; the boss, Mr Diamond; Arnold; the chef; and a waitress, and she even speaks Russian, although I know that that is not necessary. Arnold thought that it was a nice touch". He opened his smartphone and sent a message. The three Europeans' phones beeped".

"What...?" said Ivan.

"We are in a private WhatsApp group. I just sent you the address of a private printer in the main office on a different floor. I will get you your own, but if you send anything to that printer, mark it with the word 'Reaper', and a copy will be brought up to you. I'll have pens and paper sent immediately too. I'll leave you to it".

"Erm, John. Here is a list of my wife's requirement for home schooling".

"Thanks. I'll get someone onto that right away".

∞

At nine am, the European team of four started work in earnest. The food had been placed in the fridge, all signs of it having been used as a dining room had been removed, and the project books, exercise books note pads and desk diaries had been delivered.

"Our first problem, is that we know nothing about this firm. We can see from its website, and by its global reputation, that it is massive, but we don't know how many people access it on average per minute or its probable peek requirement.". He made a note under the title of 'Questions to be asked'.

They quickly brain-stormed all the questions they needed answers to immediately. It was a relatively simple task, because they had recently passed through this stage in

Belarus. They were finished by noon, and moved to the 'front' of the room near to the fridges to have a drink and await their lunch. Ivan called Sonya to suggest that it might be more conducive to creating a productive environment, if she and the children took their lunch either in their room or in the roof garden.

After lunch, Ivan idly copied up his list of questions that needed answering; Eduard made a list of peripherals that it would be useful to have at hand; Alex typed up Ivan's original list in rough into a word-processor, and Katya, who had the neatest handwriting entered the list into the desk diary under the title:

LLM AI Development Team

Developing a large language model (LLM) such as we assume you require, subject to a greater understanding of your company's specific requirements, typically calls for a sizeable, multi-disciplinary team. A project of the scale that we envisage you may need might require around 100-200 people or more, depending on the resources available and the desired capabilities of the model. Here follows a breakdown of the types of rôles involved and the size of the teams:

1. Machine Learning Engineers and Research Scientists:
This core group is essential for designing and training the model. They experiment with architectures, train the model

on large datasets, and refine algorithms. This group can vary widely, from 20 to 50+ specialists, depending on the project's complexity.

2. Data Engineers and Data Scientists:

To ensure the model has high-quality and diverse data, data engineers manage, pre-process, and scale the data pipeline. This group may also develop or refine datasets for specific model requirements, consisting of 10 to 30 team members.

3. Software Engineers:

Responsible for integrating the model with applications and optimizing performance on hardware. This team often includes front-end and back-end developers, typically around 20-40 engineers, especially for projects intended for a consumer-facing product.

4. Product Managers and Project Managers:

These rôles guide the direction and priorities of the project, ensuring it aligns with company goals and user needs. A typical project has several managers, ranging from 5-15.

5. Ethics and Responsible AI Specialists:

An LLM requires careful monitoring to avoid biases, safety risks, and ethical pitfalls. A smaller team, typically 5-10 people, focuses on ethical and regulatory issues and advises on deploying and managing the model responsibly.

6. Infrastructure and DevOps:

Managing the cloud infrastructure, scaling, and deployment is essential in an LLM project. Around 10-20 people may work on managing GPU/TPU clusters and optimising the training environment.

7. User Experience (UX) Researchers and Designers:

For an LLM that interacts with users, a dedicated team of UX researchers and designers ensures usability and intuitiveness. This team may include 5-10 individuals.

8. Quality Assurance (QA) and Testing:

To ensure reliable outputs, QA engineers and testers run multiple checks on the model's accuracy, reliability, and security. This team may range from 5-15 people.

The overall team size depends heavily on the project's scope, timeline, and budget, but it is common to see 100-200+ team members involved in a production-level LLM project similar to the one that the Russian Skolkovo Institute of Science and Technology - or Skoltech for short — is building.

Signed:
Dated:

When John arrived with Melanie and Suzanne at three o'clock, the Europeans were surprised, but very happy to find that that they would be working with people they already knew and liked, and the Americans were impressed with the detail of the list of personnel that might be required. John took the list of questions and promised answers by nine the following day.

That evening was a long one for Melanie, as the Director of Information Technology Infrastructure; Suzanne, as the Director of Talent Management; and John as the Director of Research and Development, and now official Reaper Project Team Leader.

"Congratulations on your new appointment, John!" said Melanie. "You're perfect for the job".

"I agree", said Suzanne.

"Thanks, but what you really mean is that you're glad he didn't give the job to you. I know. It's a poisoned chalice of a job. No extra pay, loads of headaches and a massive deadline to beat the competition by putting Reaper into production, so that Jim can sell it on to other companies, including the Military Industrial Complex and the Intelligence Services before anyone else can. He has promised big annual bonuses for all concerned, if we can pull it off though.

"Imagine what a product like this could be worth on a global level... Once Reaper gets out of its box, everyone will have to have it just to maintain their current status quo, and by coaxing Ivan and his friends over to us, we have thrown a spanner into Russia's attempt to become the world leader in AI technology, which they were – probably still are, but not for much longer...

"Anyway, let's get on with it. You've had time to study Ivan's shopping list of personnel, what do you think?"

They both looked at Suzanne.

"Well, as you know, we are already successful in e-commerce, logistics, and cloud services but are not yet involved in AI, so it would seem likely that we already have some team members that could be repurposed for LLM development.

"Do you want the full list, John?"

"Yes, you might as well give it me now verbally, but I will obviously need a full report for the file and him upstairs". They smiled at his reference to the boss.

"Suzanne began to read from their notes:

1] Data Engineers and Data Scientists: we have robust data teams managing supply chain analytics, customer insights, and predictive analytics for their platforms. While these engineers and scientists might need upskilling in AI-specific preprocessing or model-specific data handling, this group is already well-positioned to contribute. Mel and I estimate that the available team size is 10-20% of what's needed So, this department requires considerable growth.

2] Software Engineers: we have a focus on scalable architecture and customer applications, so we have software engineers adept at building back-end systems, web interfaces, and scalable platforms. While integration with AI systems might be new, much of their skill set would translate. We estimate the available team size to be 50-70%, depending on the internal cloud-focused or application-driven projects.

3] Product and Project Managers: our product teams focus on logistics, e-commerce features, and customer experience. Our managers are familiar with new initiatives and some could adapt to oversee an AI project, though the ethical and technical nuances of AI would require hiring or training.

"The estimated available team size is 70-80%, with some rôles transitioning to AI oversight.

4] Infrastructure and DevOps: we have an excellent, well-established e-commerce platform, so we already have significant infrastructure teams focused on uptime, security, and scalability. Their expertise in cloud management and deployment should allow for an easier transition into managing the computing resources required for AI training.

Estimated available team size: Close to 100%, though additional hires may be needed to handle GPU/TPU cluster management.

5] UX Researchers and Designers: our UX teams primarily focus on making shopping experiences seamless. However, conversational AI interfaces would require designers experienced in natural language processing (NLP) usability, meaning largish gaps in this area.

Estimated available team size: 30-50%, thus requiring new hires or collaboration with AI specialists.

6] Quality Assurance (QA) and Testing: our QA team for the e-commerce systems is highly skilled, but doesn't have experience in the linguistic and probabilistic testing necessary for an LLM. Significant upskilling or hiring would be required.

Estimated available team size: 40-60%.

"And finally, it is our professional judgement that My Media, with its existing focus on logistics, customer interfaces, and cloud services, has many of the foundational rôles needed for an LLM project. However, specialisation in AI, particularly in data preparation, ethics, and NLP-specific QA, would necessitate significant hiring or upskilling.

"We have identified three key areas for immediate expansion:

1] Machine Learning Engineers and Research Scientists: Start from scratch.

2] Ethics and Responsible AI Specialists: New hires or collaborations with academia.

3] NLP-focused QA and UX: Targeted recruitment required.

"This all boils down to us already having approximately 40-50% of the required team rôles, but we will need significant extra resources to build out AI-specific capacities".

Suzanne gave a little bow, and the others applauded silently. "Well done both. I'll get that over to Jim this evening. Will you send it to my house when you have typed it up into a report? I'm finally going home tonight".

Suzanne looked at Mel, who said, "There is something that we would like to point out, John, and it is imperative that

Jim understands it. We have a fantastic I.T. team, but it is fully occupied with the business as it stands. The figures show that you can poach a few bods from their existing jobs, and transfer them to Reaper, but only at the cost of the projects that they are working on already.

"They are great guys, and they would do anything we ask of them including pulling rabbits out of hats, but one thing they cannot do is create more hours in a day. There are twenty-four now and ever more shall be. We have always had great industrial relations with them too, so we don't want to push them to the point where we risk losing that goodwill".

"I understand, ladies. I do, really. It is an extremely valid point".

"We are sure that you do, John, but you are closer to operations than Jim is. You need to make him know these facts too, or Reaper could ruin what we already have".

"Yes, I will make sure that he understands that. Don't worry. Your concerns are locked in", he said tapping his right temple.

"We are going to have to hire another 100-200 I.T. staff eventually. There is no escaping that fact. Perhaps on short-term contracts until we see which jobs can be merged… If Jim wants to penny-pinch, my best guess is that we will need about 150 more staff within the next couple of weeks, and when we see the lay of the land, we may be able to let 50 of them go".

John made a few notes in the note pad that he always carried in his pocket, but it was more to reassure his colleagues than to prevent him from forgetting it.

"I've got a ride home booked for about now, so I had better get going. Please let me have those staff shortage figures in writing, because when I speak to Jim tonight, I am sure that he will ask me to send them to him. I hope that I can have your full report tomorrow, say, sometime before lunch.

"Thanks for the superlative work, but I really do have to run now, because my wife's patience is not boundless – generous, but not bottomless".

11: Reaper Takes to the Air!

After John had appraised him of the state of Reaper in its earliest stages, Jim worked with lightening speed. He didn't know, but he was quite certain that Reaper could soon be at the front of the race to be the first commercially-available LLM AI application in the world, and if that were not exactly true, because there was a lot of secrecy surrounding Russian, Chinese and British projects of a similar nature, his was looking good to be the first American version.

He also took some pleasure from the fact that he had added Russia's top AI designer to his team, something that would certainly set their goals back, according to Ivan. Apparently, Ivan and Eduard were at the pinnacle of the top Russian team, and were only on loan to Belarus for a very short time to get their AI project started. Much like they had just done at My Media. It was Putin's way of thanking Belarus for its support with their venture in The Ukraine.

Apparently, Putin was furious that Ivan had been smuggled out from under his nose at such a crucial point in the project, and was making terrible vows on Ivan's future, if their paths should ever cross again.

Jim had had Ivan appraised of his company's transactional data, and the recruitment drive was going to plan. Suzanne had launched an aggressive campaign to recruit the staff that Ivan deemed to be vital. So far, she was doing an excellent job of hiring people just before he needed them, meaning that the project continued smoothly and with pace. They often had to swap staff around. Experienced staff long on the My Media team might shift over to Reaper to be replaced by new recruits. Especially on sensitive placements.

Jim was keeping a close eye on the figures, and Reaper was horrendously expensive, but it was still broadly within the allocated budget, and it was in advance of expectations. In a way, though, it didn't matter because the rewards for winning the race were so astronomical.

Pinching Ivan out from under the Russians' noses, stealing a march on his rivals, the thought of the riches that he stood to make, and the cut and thrust of the operation – the excitement that he had been missing for a while - made Jim a very happy man.

Jim still hadn't been to the depot in the Santa Cruz Mountains, which were located to the south of Silicon Valley, not far from Palo Alto, where he lived, to meet his new team. However, that was because his advisors had warned him that there was still a possibility of repercussions from their defection. They convinced him by asking whether he normally went to meet a team of workers just because they had been recently recruited, and it was true that he didn't.

He did, however usually present an award to the group, which had made the most money per head every year, and he did often do that in person. If Reaper were ready by the new year, it could easily be the top earner, and then a visit from the boss would not be unusual. He had heard that the 'Russians', as he thought of them, had come to grips with speaking English remarkably quickly, but he still didn't relish the prospect of having halting conversations with people he didn't know, and who were, at the end of the day, just employees – people he was paying very well to do a job for him.

Jim wasn't a bad person, but he was a bit of a snob and an elitist. He valued his staff and employees, but he did not consider them his equals. There was no way that he would invite anyone below the rank of a senior board member to his home. In fact, none of the current board had ever been invited to his retreat in Palo Alto, but then most of them were fairly young, and also recent appointments.

It had been different in 'the old days', meaning before he had become a billionaire. Back then, he was still pretty close to some of his staff – especially the people he worked with every day, but these days, he had his fingers in so many pies; he was talking to dozens of people all over the world every day, and, although he didn't like to admit it, he was getting old. What's more, there was something that he had overheard one of his rivals once say that resonated with him, but which he would never speak out loud. He was ashamed that he liked it. It was that he now had 'Sod off money'. It meant that if anyone didn't like the way he treated them, they could sod off, because he didn't have to worry what anyone thought of him any more… with the exception of only his immediate family.

Three people were the only living creatures in the whole world that mattered to him.: his wife, and his two daughters, who were both in their thirties, and both of whom he hardly ever saw. He did have the perspicacity to blame himself for that though, because when they were growing up, he had spent more time at work than he had with them. It was just about the only thing that he regretted in his whole life, and it had been known to bring him to tears.

He made a note to himself to tell John to tell Arnold on the QT that his unit was neck and neck to win the Annual Productivity Prize the following year, and that he would surely win, if his people could just do a little better.

They would win – there was no doubt of that because a 'compensatory amount' would be added for the Reaper Team, and he would ensure that it was just enough to win the competition. It was the way the game was played, he thought to himself and smiled.

Jim had always thought of himself as a Machiavelli.

∞

"The Europeans", as they came to be known, were given everything they needed in the way of equipment and personnel. No expense was spared, which caused some friction from department heads who were not being kept in the loop with what Reaper was about. Everybody in the complex knew that The Europeans existed 'on the top floor', and that their existence was supposed to be a secret, because they were working on a 'highly sensitive new project'. The caterers and the cleaners could vouch for that, but it was still a secret, for the first few weeks at least, what they were working on.

However, it became increasingly difficult to conceal the importance and the identity of the new project when the number of staff started to increase. One day, John told Jim that it was no longer feasible to keep Project Reaper a secret.

For the first time ever, John was invited around to Jim's home office. He parked his car in the basement, and took the direct lift to Jim's observatory-office on the roof of his house.

"Yes, John, I understand that completely. In fact, I have been waiting for you to give me the exact same message that you just did. I was just waiting to the last possible minute. You've done… you are doing, a great job, John, and that won't go unrewarded – you can believe me on that one. It is time to tell the staff at the Santa Cruz Mountains' depot something about what is going on 'upstairs'. I'll leave the exact release date to you, but hold the info back as long as you can… to the last second, and impress on them that divulging what you are telling them is a sackable offence under the Industrial Espionage Act.

"I'm not sure whether it is or not, or even whether that's the name of the act, but it doesn't matter. Say it anyway… False news has become acceptable these days – facts no longer seem to matter. It's all about feelings and emotions these days. If anyone wants to be a smart ass, refer them to Donald in the legal department. He'll baffle them with so much bullshit that they won't remember what their objection was. He's a great waffler, Donald. Do you know him?"

"No, sir. I don't think that I do…"

"Big man, small hands. He's a better bullshitter than a lawyer, but then again, how much difference is there?

"The point is, or the most important point is, that we have to bring the Reaper Project staff more into the light. The team is too big to hide now even in the Santa Cruz Mountains, so we have to hide them behind a name.

"We have decided to call the team and the project it is developing "Camelot". I like it because there's a lot riding on it! Get it? It will get people guessing, and that's OK. While they are distracted with guessing what it all means, we will be making it all happen.

"John, let's have a drink on the fantastic job that you, Melanie and Suzanne put in motion last month in Warsaw, and that your wider team is now grappling". Jim pushed a glass of Laphroaig single malt towards him. "You're a good man, John. Keep it up.

"What do you think of my office, John? First time you've been up here, I think", he said knowing that it was the first time he had ever set foot in his grounds, leave alone his private space.

"It is truly inspiring, sir – even awe-inspiring. We have a nice property in the Valley, but the street light pollution makes seeing the stars impossible… I haven't seen them for years… so long that I've stopped looking up".

"Yes, that's sad, but never stop looking up, John, it's the only place to go. Onwards, and upwards! Eh? Onwards and upwards! 'Onwards and downwards!' ? That would be a ridiculous thing to say, wouldn't it? Come on, let me top you up.

"I have spoken to Arnold about housing our new staff – the Reaper Staff… I don't mean providing them with houses, I mean office space. It seems that the Santa Cruz Mountains depot is fit to burst. I have authorised him to rent however many portacabins he needs. The Reaper staff will be put in them. If we shifted our more core staff into them for the sake of the Reaper staff, I think we would be causing problems…"

"I agree, sir".

"Good! It is best if we are all singing from the same hymn sheet. I have also authorised him to build a proprietary Camelot Block alongside the current one. It should have interconnecting access to encourage homogeneity – so that everyone feels part of the same team – Team My Media".

"I couldn't agree more, sir. We are at full capacity at the Santa Cruz Mountains depot, but we still have about fifty recruitments to make".

They discussed the project until late into the night, and them John drove home knowing that he was way over the limit. Jim made a note on his personal personnel file of this reckless, inconsiderate side of his favourite employee.

Who knew when such a piece of personally-gained information might come in useful? he thought. No-one had access to the private records of his personal observations on the characters of every important person in his life. It included members of his family, his top staff at My Media, important people that he had met and even presidents of the United States and their top-level staff. In short, he had his own personal CIA-type file on anyone who could affect his business for good or ill.

∞

Two months after Project Reaper had been officially launched by the installation of Ivan and his team, it was ready to test drive. The monster application was not finished by a long chalk, but it was functioning on a low level It wasn't ready to go live-live, but it was sort of operational – it was more or less in the test zone, and that created an atmosphere of tense exuberance.

Jim was keen to meet the Reaper team, but he still didn't want to draw attention to it, so he agreed to open the new Camelot Block when it was ready. It was a pretty basic , rendered concrete block, two storey construction, but it had been build with future upward expansion in mind.

Calling the hand-over a topping out ceremony was rather grand, but that's how it was billed to make it sound important enough for the CEO of an international conglomerate to open it in person.

They were fortunate with the weather, so Jim gave a speech to the staff, who were assembled on the tarmac before him. He talked of a bright future for My Media, which meant job-security for its staff and continuing annual increases in salary, and where appropriate, bonuses. As evidence of My Media's continuing prosperity, he pointed to the recent large increase in staff and the need for a new building for them to work in.

"What more concrete evidence of the permanence of your jobs could there be than the new Camelot Block? May all who work in her be happy, healthy, prosperous and productive. I now declare the Camelot Block open and ready for business!" whereupon he pulled on the rope that drew the red curtain hanging before the entrance. Jim descended from the dais, and entered the building, where the caterers had arranged a buffet and bar

He shook hands and exchanged pleasantries with dozens of people including Ivan for thirty minutes, then asked John to show him and Ivan to the meeting room upstairs, so they could have a chat.

"Well, Ivan, it's good to finally get to have a few words with you. John speaks very highly of you and your European team. Are you fitting in with us Americans too?"

"How should I address you?"

"Er, you can call me Jim, er today…"

"Very well, Jim. It is nice to meet you too. Yes, we are are happy to be working here, but the environment is rather restrictive on my wife and children. It is a concern".

"Yes. I can imagine. Well, you are in a rather complicated predicament. If you come up with a solution, I'll be happy to listen to it. Now, as for Reaper. Where are we now?"

"I am happy to be able to tell you that we have a prototype – a very early, clumsy one, but it works. However, you are looking for a genius sprinter, and what we have is an ingenue baby – clever, even brilliant, but it knows nothing and is still crawling on all fours. You could say that it is like the British Library without any books".

Jim looked puzzled. "Well, let's stock our library with books!" he looked around to judge whether he had made a fool of himself.

"Quite so, Jim. That is our next task. You will now be wondering where we get the books. We, or you really, Jim, have three choices: 1] Get Beta testers; 2] Go public; and 3] A mixture of 1] and 2]. Let me make a suggestion. First, how many employees do you have worldwide?"

"A million and a half? About that, eh John?" John nodded.

"How many search queries do they all make in a day?"

"I have no way of knowing that , Ivan. Come on, now!"

"It was a rhetorical question, but let's assume five each. They could be looking up anything… spelling, grammar, stuff to do with, work, hobbies, restaurants, bus or train timetables, et cetera, et cetera. That makes seven and a half million queries a day! If you go public, you will get more queries more quickly, but you will also receive many complaints, and that may have an adverse effect on your company's image".

"So, how do we make them use Reaper?"

"We simply make Reaper the default search engine on all company devices, and we reroute or rather duplicate queries to other search engines to Reaper. To be safer, we should provide two answers to every question: Reaper's reply and the one from the search engine they originally queried. Finally, we can send all that data back here for it to be analysed. This method will put books on the shelves of your library, and tell you what staff are using your computers for when they are and when they are not working".

"I like it!" he said clapping Ivan on the back. "You said he was smart and you were god-damn right! How long before the library is full, Ivan?"

"We don't know, is the answer, Jim. Remember that song: 'There are more questions than answers'? That is because every answer raises at least one more question. So, in theory, it can never know everything, and if the library becomes full, we can build extensions to house more books. Not only that, but we are in advance now of where I left the Russian project. I think that you have the most advanced LLM AI system in the world". Jim's utter delight was evident on his face as he beamed joy to the faces around him. It was like he was the first of his circle at school to get a racing bike or an air rifle.

"Would you like to implement option one, Jim?"

"Yes. I think that's the way to go. Let's not waste any time!"

"Very well. One minute, please…" There was a company laptop on a trolley before every seat at the large table, he pulled one towards him switched it on, logged into his personal Reaper Developer's account, and said, "Do you want to switch it on personally, Jim?"

"You bet, I do!"

"Click that green button with the mouse, and Reaper will be implemented on all company computers worldwide. It may take an hour to propagate, but it will happen before we get home today". Jim reached over, moved the cursor to the green box, looked around the faces of those assembled there a little anxiously, and clicked the button. The half-a-dozen people in the room clapped and cheered, as Reaper took flight.

"Let's go and have a beer, guys!" said Jim.

12: Learning to Fly

The various My Media managers around the world were simply told that the company was developing its own search engine. They were also told to expect a higher number of complaints than normal from users, and odd, to incorrect results from the search engine as it was 'learning its job'. All company staff were advised to go with the results from their usual search engine, if Reaper's reply looked wrong, and to click the check box by the result that they had accepted as accurate.

Ivan was glued to the screen in his new office in the Camelot Block, fascinated by the amount of data that was streaming in. He had suggested that there might be 7,500,000 queries per day, but there were twice to three times that amount, It amazed him how little savvy most employees had. They seemed completely unaware that their searches were being logged, which meant that Ivan could see which computer in which office had originated a search, at what time of the day, and what they were searching for.

There was so much online shopping going on during working hours and even searches for porn sites. It was none of his concern, but he thought that Jim would be interested to know. The question was whether he wanted to be the one to tell him. It was easy enough to deter. Known shopping and porn site URL's could be diverted to a Big Brother type warning page with a message designed to scare the bejesus out of the searcher. Something like:

"We have noticed that you are using this company computer for your own gratification during office hours

"A report has been sent to the office manager!"

There were a couple of surprises in the global metadata that was coming in though. 1] There were not as many complaints as he had expected. People seemed very happy, even excited to be taking part is such a global experiment. They were making history. 2] It was taking longer than he had expected to 'fill the library'. Even with the answers to up to 20 millions queries a day coming in, it was still going too slowly for him, and so would definitely be going too slowly for Jim.

The 'problem' seemed to be that people all over the world were asking the same type of questions such as what is thirty-six inches in metric? What is number one in the pop charts? What is the best-selling film? What time is the bus or flight? How many dollars to the pound sterling? How can I lose weight? What is a good work-from-home job? Plus the inevitable queries about shopping and pornography.

It was all, or mostly, rather mundane.

When Ivan mentioned his concerns to his boss, John had a brainwave. They had a media company with access to the literature of the world in almost every language, and not only literature, but also school books, maths courses, teach-yourself books, including languages, and self-help books. They had the whole gamut! Reaper could devour a 'Teach Yourself Russian' book in minutes, and hey presto! a computer that could read and write in Russian. Even speak it! It could learn every language and every discipline that man was interested in as quickly as they could feed the data into it. They had already started their own Gutenberg Project, but is was not being taken seriously. Now they could change its focus. They could even download digital copies of the old masters from Gutenberg and feed them into Reaper.

The revelation was enlightening, and the two men knew immediately that it would be a shot in the arm for their project. John sought Jim's approval, and got it although he came away from the meeting with the impression that Jim had not grasped what a leap forward this would mean.

The Library Team, which was their equivalent to Gutenberg was quadrupled in size and given overtime. John came to look at Reaper like Pac-Man gobbling up any, and everything that was placed before it. There was no stopping Reaper now. It could code apps in seconds, work out rocket trajectories, and discuss any book in any language.

There came a day, when Ivan said that Reaper could handle its own education from then on, but that they had to teach it about pictures, or images, and speech. The Reaper team brainstormed ideas for how to teach their baby how to recognise images. Suggestions ranged from photo competitions, through reading the daily paper to watching films with subtitles. They set about trials to find out which method wold work the best the most quickly. They already had hundreds of thousands of films on DVD's and in the Cloud.

It seemed that subtitled films worked the best, but first Reaper had to be taught the basics, like the difference in shape between a cat and a dog. Once it had these basic images, it could probably work out the rest from the subtitles.

Another team set about giving Reaper a repertoire of 'humanoid' voices, which didn't sound robotic. This was somewhat easier, because Reaper could match the voices of the actors in the films to the subtitles. The team was building up quite a variety of celebrity cloned voices, for which Jim and the sales teams were trying to work out a sellable use.

∞

While Reaper was going from victory to victory, although it was still being explained away as just another 'search engine', the home lives of the Europeans had improved too with the new block. Four new homes had been incorporated into it. Three 'terraced' houses on the ground floor at the back of the building looking into the forest that surrounded them, so that the aircraft would not bother them too much, and a suite on the roof which was typical of every My Media office block. Ivan and his family moved into the penthouse suite complete with its roof garden. The views were terrific and subdued the feelings of imprisonment that had been blighting the lives of Sonya and the girls.

However, all the Europeans longed to be able to get off their mountain and visit the valley below. It had been almost three months since they had arrived and Christmas was drawing near.

One morning, Ivan said, "John, a word, please. Do you realise that Russians give Christmas gifts on St Nicholas' Day, 6th December, not on Christmas day? It would be such a wonderful surprise for my family and colleagues to be able to take a trip to a department store before then". John had promised to ask Jim, but when they had not received an answer by the 4th December, Ivan was determined to ask again. Hours later John phoned Ivan with the good news. "A limousine will be available to take the seven of you to the nearest town tomorrow at ten am. Do you have cash or cards?"

"No, the cards haven't arrived yet, but we do have bank accounts".

"OK, no problem. I'll get seven My Media pre-paid bank cards made up for you. Will a thousand dollars in each one be enough for now. You can have what you want, but this isn't a gift, it'll be deducted from your salaries".

"It's plenty, thank you, John".

"The limo will take you to Macy's in Stanford Shopping Center. You can wander around, but let our security take care of you. I mean if someone tries to talk to you, refer them to your security detail. We don't want anyone getting suspicious about you.

"You will be travelling in a My Media limousine, which will impress people, although they are used to seeing visiting dignitaries. You don't work for us, you are just visiting Jim and our operation for possible future co-operation. OK?

"Have a great time – the car is yours all day. Say hello to the girls for me, they're great kids".

∞

Doing normal things like shopping for clothes, food, and accessories was a fantastic tonic for the 'Europeans', especially Ivan's daughters, although none of them had ever been to the West before. They were amazed at the level of choice, stunned by the prices, but in awe of the $1,000 that they had to spend. It was more than ten times the highest amount that they had ever had before. At first, they were tempted to think that the dream they were in could not last, so it would be better to keep the money – only spend a small proportion of it, but when they confided these thoughts in Ivan, he told them to 'spend, spend, spend', because they had hit the jackpot, and would be able to write their own salary cheques from then on.

The advice was true, but they hadn't been brought up to be self-indulgent spendthrifts, so they only spent half of the money, and spent most of that on their colleagues and the two teenage girls.

The four adults were in no doubt about their future earnings ability, although they too felt that 'it was just too good to be true'. Their only regrets were that they were illegal; that they couldn't tell their loved ones 'back home' that they were safe and well; and that they couldn't share their prosperity with them just yet. If they ever would be able to.

Ivan asked his security detail whether there was a good Russian restaurant in the area, and they were taken to 'Bevri' which, she assured them, was considered an up-market restaurant that offered authentic Georgian cuisine.

They chose khachapuri and khinkali amongst other dishes, and were treated like royalty, probably because of their ability to speak Russian, the date, the security detail and the huge limousine that was parked outside

All of 'the Europeans' concluded that that was the best shopping trip that they had ever had, and that the meal, and the accompanying music was superb. It brought tears to the eyes of all the adults, but not the girls.

When their trip 'outside' was over, and they were back in their new home on the distribution centre, they all felt that they could make a go of living and working in America. There had been a culture shock, and being isolated to the centre was not ideal for them, but this trip had shown them that they could integrate and enjoy what America had to offer.

As an additional treat, Ivan was determined to secure the right for the Europeans to wander in the woods that surrounded them. It was a forest really, but Russians had a long history of enjoying wandering in woods or forests, looking for wild strawberries, mushrooms, nuts and the like. He was sure that they would not be denied the simple pleasure of foraging as a family or as a group of friends.

Ivan phoned John in the late afternoon when they were back home and thanked him for arranging the best day that the seven of them had enjoyed for years. He didn't mention the foraging, or even his surprise idea of building a dacha in the woods. It was the historical dream of most Russians to one day own a dacha, but after the concessions that they had received that day, he thought that it would be better received another time.

He wished that his dearly departed parents could see him and his family. They had always been good to him, but had died young in a car crash. He actually believed that they could see him, but was used to saying what was expected of him in an atheist country, so as not to make enemies, and smooth his path upwards. It was the only aspect about himself that made him feel weak.

∞

The project was nearing it's closed testing phase. It had also consumed thousands of books, and, in theory at least could now read and write in every language in the world that was being taught in school. It was incorrect to think that it could learn no more from beta testing, but the rate of progress would be too slow. It now needed to be tested for robustness when being used by the general public, which was the class of users least likely to know how to use the new tool. It was common knowledge that so few people ever bothered to read the instructions of anything they used. Scholars and manufacturers' surveys had proved it time and time again.

Joe Public was by far the best stress-tester of any item destined for use by the general public. Ivan explained this to John at their next meeting, and he understood the principles.

"I can see why you would want to take Reaper live, Ivan, but could you explain to me the signposts that Reaper has passed to make you come to this decision?"

"Yes, I could do that, John, but it a lengthy and somewhat complicated explanation. Please don't misunderstand me, but I would rather go through the process only once. Therefore, would it be possible for you to arrange a meeting with Jim and whoever else he deems should be present? As soon as possible would be best, if we are to maintain our lead over the competitors".

"In your personal opinion, who do you think our competitors are – solely in this project, I mean?"

"In my opinion, LLM AI is probably following the same general trajectory as the Atomic Bomb. In its earliest stages, the American and British governments together with their military units collaborated to create the first Atomic Bomb. However, there were also other governments working on their own versions of the project in secret too, such as Germany and the USSR. China, Japan, the UK, and the EU governments are probably working on AI too. Russia definitely is. The difference is that you have co-opted me into your private company, and as far as I know, I am the world's most advanced AI technician. You will win the AI race because foreigners helped you.

"Just as the United States won the atomic race because foreigners helped them. You don't believe me?

"J. Robert Oppenheimer, was a Jewish-American genius, fair enough, but his four top, indispensable colleagues were all European: Enrico Fermi, born in Rome; Leo Szilard, born in Budapest, Niels Bohr, born in Copenhagen, and Edward Teller, also born in Budapest.

"It is nothing to get upset about. I am simply dealing with facts, as I do every minute of my working day".

John nodded. "I'll get back to you on that meeting", he said, and left the room.

13: Flying Solo

When John and Ivan were called into Jim's office the following afternoon, they were not surprised to find him alone. Secrecy was still important right up to the last moment. They had arrived by helicopter from Camelot minutes before solely to attend the meeting.

"I'm going to treat this meeting as informal, mainly because nobody really understands this thing we, you, have created – not even our, er, Director of Information Technology Infrastructure, Melanie Marshall, whom I think you know, Ivan. Perhaps, I should have let her sit in on this… Ivan, make sure you get typed up whatever it is you are going to explain to us this morning, and get a copy over to Melanie ASAP."

"Certainly, Jim". The hairs on the back of Jim's neck bristled on hearing his name, but he said nothing. "Will you take care of that, John?"

"Certainly, sir", he said rather pointedly.

"No need to call me 'sir', John. This is an informal meeting for the purpose of disseminating information among colleagues only. Would anyone like a drink of anything. He looked at his watch. I know it's a little early, but the sun will soon be over the yardarm".

John knew Jim's expressions well enough to know that Jim's yardarm was anytime between three and four pm. He often used nautical expressions. "I'll have whatever you're having, Jim", said John."

"A bottle of cold beer and a vodka chaser, please" said Ivan to Jim's enquiring look.

"Cheers", they all said clinking glasses. "To Reaper, and all who sail in her", added Jim. "OK, let's have it, Ivan".

"Very well. An LLM AI system, such as ours, should, in my opinion, be considered "good enough" to go live for the general public when it meets a range of technical, ethical, and operational criteria. The key factors include:

1. Performance Benchmarks

• Accuracy and Relevance: The model consistently generates correct, relevant, and contextually appropriate responses across diverse queries.

• Robustness: It handles edge cases, ambiguous prompts, and diverse language inputs effectively.

• Evaluation Metrics: Metrics like BLEU scores for language generation quality or human-rated satisfaction scores must surpass predefined thresholds, which they are doing.

2. Safety and Ethical Compliance

• Bias Mitigation: Extensive testing must ensure minimal biases in responses across sensitive topics like gender, race, or religion. Our team is satisfied that this is the case.

- Toxicity Filtering: The system is trained or fine-tuned to avoid generating harmful, offensive, or misleading content. Our team is satisfied that this is the case.

- Regulatory Compliance: It adheres to privacy laws and any region-specific regulations. Perhaps legal ought to be the judge of this.

3. User Experience

- Ease of Use: The interface and interaction design should be intuitive and user-friendly. They are.

- Customisability: Users can easily adjust settings for tone, depth, or specificity where applicable. These settings are in place.

4. Infrastructure Readiness

- Scalability: the infrastructure must be able handle high traffic without compromising performance. We are easily handling our current workload.

- Real-Time Capability: Latency has to be low enough for seamless user interaction. It is.

5. Extensive Testing

- Alpha and Beta Testing: Internal tests have been followed by controlled public rollouts to gather real-world feedback. We are on track.

- Stress Tests: The system has to have been tested under heavy usage to ensure stability. This is why we have to go live in order to improve.

6. Operational Viability

- Cost-Efficiency: Running costs for hardware, cloud services, and maintenance must be manageable relative to the projected user base. This is not my decision.

- Monitoring Systems: Tools to track errors, performance metrics, and user feedback must be in place for post-launch support. They are.

7. Public Trust

- Transparency: Users are informed about the model's capabilities and limitations. This is already being done.

- Privacy Safeguards: Data collection policies are clear and respectful of user privacy. So it this.

"I believe that the transition to general public availability should follow extensive internal validation and controlled public trials such as beta launches, which we achieved through testing Reaper on My Media staff throughout the globe.

"I and my team believe that Reaper has passed that stage now because of those rollouts with limited access. Now is the time for broader public deployment to refine the system based on real-world usage and feedback. My opinion has been reached after consultation with our Quality Assurance and Testing department".

"Any questions?" he asked, sipping his beer from the bottle.

"Er, John, any questions for Ivan? Did you understand all that?"

"No, I don't have any immediate questions, but yes, I did understand it. I don't think I could repeat it though".

"No, nor me. Ivan, hand me the sheets you were reading that data from. I'll make a few copies". He used his office copier, then gave the original back to Ivan, handed two to John, and kept one. "There's an extra copy for Melanie, John.

"Well, gentlemen, I am very impressed. You've both done a great job, and so have your teams. Ivan, two things. First, did you run this past our lawyers? And second, please get a report typed up in full ASAP".

"Erm, firstly, no I don't have any lawyers on my direct team, and when I approached the department, I was told that they worked for you, and had not received any instructions to take requests from me. Secondly, Katya has probably finished having the report typed up by now. Would you like me to check?"

"No, not now. Do it when we're finished here. John, that was an oversight not to give Ivan access to our legal team. Can you fix that? Oh, and get them to take a look at Ivan's official report. If you get it to them today, give them twenty-four hours for their verdict on whether we can turn Reaper on or not tomorrow.

"Ivan, Legal may have questions, and since I am not giving them much time, can you be available to answer their questions until this time tomorrow?"

"Yes, Jim, that is not a problem".

"OK, then, gentlemen, one quick one for the road, and it's back to work".

∞

This time Melanie was included in the meeting that was held in Jim's Board Room, as was a Robert Saunders.

"Melanie and John, you both know Bob already, but I don't think that you do, Ivan. Ivan, this is Robert Saunders our Chief Legal Officer, Robert, this is Ivan".

They shook hands. "We spoke several times this morning over the phone, Ivan. Please call me Bob, most people who know me do".

"Right let's get this meeting underway. As you all know, we are about to decide whether to turn Reaper loose on the world. Bob, did you have any concerns?"

"We put all our top people onto this yesterday, and came up with a few things. The good news is though, that Ivan had already thought of most of them and had them covered. Nevertheless, our major concerns were, and some still are, the following… er, you can follow my list on the handout from my office among the papers in front of you; they have also been copied to your inboxes. Anyway:

1. Legal and Regulatory Compliance

- Data Privacy Laws: The system must comply with data protection regulations like the GDPR (Europe) – that's the General Data Protection Regulation in Europe, and the CCPA (California), or the California Consumer Privacy Act. and similar laws worldwide. This includes how user data is collected, processed, and stored. By the way, CCPA is one one of the strictest privacy laws in America, and is rigorously enforced, while the GDPR is even worse – from our perspective of compliance, naturally. Then there's:

- Content Liability: My Media will need to address potential liabilities for harmful or misleading outputs from the AI, such as defamation, copyright violations, or spreading false information. Then there are

- Jurisdictional Challenges: Different countries have varying regulations, requiring careful monitoring to avoid legal conflicts. Er,

2. Ethical and Safety Concerns

- Bias and Discrimination: If Reaper outputs biased or discriminatory content, the company could face reputational damage and legal challenges.

●	Misinformation: We need to ensure that the system does not inadvertently spread false or harmful information. This is crucial, as it could have real-world implications.

●	User Safety: My department will need to assess risks related to Reaper providing advice on sensitive matters like health, finance, or law.

3. Intellectual Property (IP) Issues

●	Training Data: This is an ongoing problem, we must ensure that the training data does not infringe on copyrights or violate other Intellectual Property laws, but we've pretty much got that covered already.

●	Generated Content Ownership: We need to clarify whether content created by Reaper – for example text, images and speech, is owned by the company, the user, or falls into the public domain.

4. Contractual Obligations

●	Third-Party Agreements: If Reaper relies on third-party APIs, data sets, or software, we would need to review licensing agreements and usage rights.

●	User Terms of Service: The system's terms must clearly define the company's responsibilities and user liabilities.

5. Risk Management

- Global Availability: Launching Reaper globally increases exposure to legal and reputational risks, making comprehensive risk assessments critical.

- Product Liability: My department would need to consider the risk of legal claims if users rely on Reaper outputs that cause harm or financial loss.

6. Anti-trust and Competition Concerns

- Market Impact: If Reaper offers a significant competitive advantage, which it will in our opinion, regulators may scrutinise its impact on market competition.

- Monopoly Accusations: Deploying a transformative AI tool, like Reaper, globally might draw accusations of monopolistic practices, especially in highly regulated sectors.

And finally, for now at least,

7. Litigation Risks

- We need to start preparing for lawsuits from individuals, organisations, or governments concerning data misuse, biased outputs, or other unforeseen consequences.

Bob could plainly see the dismay and concern on the faces around him. He pulled a 'sorry' face and shrugged. "Sorry, guys, but those are our initial concerns. Like I said earlier, Ivan and his team have already addressed some of these issues, but those measures do need tightening up, because he is not an International lawyer, nor even an American one… and, in fact, not any kind of a lawyer.

"Here are a few actions we can take:

• Pre-Launch Testing: Mandating extensive testing to ensure compliance and mitigate risks. This is an ongoing thing that you have already started. You are in this phase now

• Legal Disclaimers: Drafting robust disclaimers about the AI's limitations. My team has drawn up a list of disclaimers that we will get to in a minute.

• Stakeholder Collaboration: Working with technical teams to address legal and ethical concerns during development. This is another aspect that is ongoing, but we will need to fine tune it, especially to comply with the European and Californian data protection and privacy laws.

• Monitoring and Response Plans: Setting up mechanisms to quickly address issues post-launch. I know that Ivan has procedures in place that can address these issues, but again, they need to be fit for purpose from a legal point of view.

"Now, that list of suggested disclaimers:

1. General Disclaimer

"This AI system is provided as is, without guarantees or warranties of any kind. Use is at your own risk."

2. Accuracy and Reliability

"The system may not always provide accurate, complete, or up-to-date information. Users should independently verify any advice or information received."

3. Not a Substitute for Professional Advice

"The AI's outputs are not intended to replace professional advice, including legal, medical, financial, or other specialised guidance. Always consult a qualified professional for specific issues."

4. Ethical and Offensive Content

"While the system is designed to minimise harmful outputs, it may occasionally generate biased, offensive, or inappropriate content. We encourage users to report such instances for review."

5. Liability Waiver

"The company is not liable for any damages resulting from the use or inability to use the system, including but not limited to indirect, incidental, or consequential damages."

6. User Data Privacy

"Interactions with the AI may be logged and reviewed to improve system performance. Refer to our Privacy Policy for more details."

7. Content Ownership

"Generated content is the sole responsibility of the user, and the company assumes no liability for its use or distribution."

8. Jurisdictional Limitations

"Use of this system must comply with local laws and regulations. Access may be restricted or modified in certain regions."

9. Beta or Evolving Nature

"This is a beta product and is under active development. Features and performance may change over time."

10. Feedback Disclaimer

"User feedback is welcomed and may be incorporated into future updates. Submission of feedback implies consent for its use by the company."

"We would like you to display these disclaimers prominently in the user agreement, app interface, and FAQ sections to ensure transparency, and protect the company from legal and reputational risks.

"For a company like My Media, the global scope and scale of such a launch make these considerations even more critical. Finally, in my capacity as CLO, I strongly advocate a phased rollout employing robust safeguards to minimise exposure to legal and reputational risks".

"Wow! If we thought that Ivan's list yesterday was mind-numbing, Bob's topped it! I'm not trying to be rude to either of you. You are top guys in your fields, this sort of talk is normal to you, but, well, I'm sure you can imagine that it's a lot – a Hell of a lot for some of us to take in. So, Bob, bottom line, can we switch it on or not?"

"I think that that has to be an operational and executive decision. I am only an advisor, a consigliere. Ivan has to decide whether Reaper is fit for purpose, and you have to decide whether you believe him, and whether you believe that you have covered the legal aspects that I have pointed out".

"In other words, you would wait".

"Lawyers are a cautious breed by nature, Jim. Fortunately, this is not my decision to make".

"You can't get a straight answer out of them either…"

"It is unwise to take decisions when one doesn't have to".

"Fair enough. It is not your decision. If I gave you another week, Bob, could you ensure that Reaper is compliant with what you just warned us against, and Ivan, same question to you. If you both work closely together, could you make a big difference in a week?"

Both men nodded. Ivan spoke first. "From my point of view, we are ready to go now, based on my Russian background. I realise that America is far more litigious, so I bow to your experience there, but the subclauses already exist in Reaper. They just need to be 'filled in' and activated. How can I put this, erm, in its simplest form, Reaper is like a flowchart with conditional questions. If this, then that…

"So, let's take the problem of country-specific legal compliance. Reaper looks at the geolocation of the inquirer. If it sees a European country then it consults option 2; if it sees USA, California, it consults option 3; Russia, option 4… as many options as you like, as many country specific disclaimers as you like. All those side shoots from the main flow-line already exist, but they are empty, and so closed off.

"If you give us something to put in option 2, for example, we will turn option 2 on. It is as simple as that for us".

"As for my department, we already comply with international law because we already operate globally, so we just have to give Ivan access to that data, so that he can plug it into Reaper, or whatever he has to do with it. As far as I am concerned, we could get a lot done in a week, and be a lot closer to being compliant".

"Ivan?"

"Once we have the data we need, we can make Reaper compliant".

"Don't look so disappointed, Ivan. Think of all the extra knowledge Reaper will have processed in a week. It will be an even better product to release to the public".

"I suppose so, Jim. Reaper handles millions of queries daily, which translates to billions of tokens…"

"What's a token?"

"Individual words or pieces of words processed in interactions…

"Yes, OK, we get the picture. So, you are agreeing with me? If Reaper processes billions of tokens a day for the next week, and you work with Bob, to make it less likely that we will get sued, we will be launching a better product?"

"Yes", he said reluctantly, "It will be".

"So, that's a 'Yes' then. Ladies and Gentlemen, you have another week. Keep me in the loop, and unless something crops up, we'll meet again in a week from now. Well done everyone. Good afternoon".

∞

The week dragged by for Ivan and his team, all of whom were disappointed that Reaper had not been switched on, but they were mostly Americans, and understood the company's need for safety. In contrast, the time flew past for the legal team, because they were worried that they may have missed something which could cause problems down the line.

Jim just rode the wave. Happy that he would be able to turn Reaper on in a week, and happier still that his product would be in better shape to inform the world and be safer from the inevitable litigants.

When the big day came, it was a formality. Jim turned Reaper on, Ivan and his team could barely tear themselves away from their monitors even to go to the bathroom, and the press office released news items, blog posts, notices, articles, and press releases predicting a Golden Age for everyone, when AI became the norm.

Jim thought that he must be the happiest man in the world, because he foresaw all major companies and even governments rushing to buy tailored copies of his Reaper at the cost of billions of dollars each.

14: Something in the Air

Niew turned the key in the front door of his house and shouted to alert his expectant wife. "Hello, Elle, it's only me".

She knew who it was because he had been saying exactly the same thing, in exactly the same way at exactly the same time since she had given up work to have their baby six weeks before. She loved the way he tried not to scare her though, and loved him too.

"OK, Niew, I'm in here", she replied acting out her rôle in the play. She stood up to wait the few seconds that it would take for him to enter the room, cross over to her and give her a kiss.

"Everything OK, my dear?" he asked on queue.

"Sure!", she replied regaining her seat at her computer desk. "How has your day been?"

They were both in their twenties, and both in I.T. They had met in Bangkok university studying I.T. and had gotten jobs in the same Bangkok giant I.T. solutions provider shortly after graduating. Elle had had to finish work early because of some problems with her pregnancy, but she still had her job to go back to when she was ready. In the meantime, she was pursuing her hobby of selling books online. It was something that had gotten her through university, because her parents were not well off, and she had been selling books ever since.

"I'll make us a cup of camomile tea", he said, as he did every evening.

"The water has boiled", she shouted after hm on cue.

When Niew returned bearing the two cups of tea on a tray, he also brought the only genuine surprise of the play. "What have we got today?"

"Apfelstrudel".

Niew studied his wife's beautiful face, and thought that she looked tired. "Did anything happen today, my dear? You look a bit... I don't know... sort of worn out".

"Nah... it's nothing, Niew. Just some sort of glitch with two of my clients' accounts".

"What? Come on, do tell?"

"Well, two of the authors whose books I help to sell have reported that My Media is threatening to close their accounts unless they can prove that they wrote some of their books".

"How do you mean 'prove that they wrote some of their books'?"

"Well, that's the point. The five books in question have been on sale at My Media for six, seven, eight years, and there has never been a problem before... but now today, they want proof! These authors are asking me how they can prove that they wrote their books so many years ago. I can't think of a way. Can you? It's like proving that you ate an apple six years ago – it's just not possible".

"No. Weird, eh? I haven't said anything before, but we've been getting weird responses from some client queries that we have been asking of our search engine. We automatically assumed that those clients had been hacked, but it now looks like they haven't been.

"Look, this is top secret, OK. Well, it is only a rumour, but it has come from Chuay, so most people believe it. He has said not to spread this rumour, but I can trust you. I know that… You love and respect our boss Chuay as much as I do – he asks after you every day, you know. Well, Chuay said that several giant American companies are developing AI systems like no-one has ever imagined before".

"What sort of AI? What is its function?"

"Nobody knows that, but it seems that they want it to be the font of all knowledge… Wait, how did Chuay put it… The Repository of all Knowledge – instantly accessible and interactive".

Elle's eyes lit up. "But what is wrong with that? It sounds fantastic! I can't wait to access it!"

"True, my love. The only downside that Chuay can see is that this giant AI is only a baby at the moment, and, like all babies…" he said rubbing his wife's tummy, it needs to be trained. Just like our little monkey will need to be trained otherwise he or she will cause havoc in our lives. Chuay said that this AI Giant is so vast, and its tentacles so invasive that it is possible that it will be a little disruptive in the short term. Perhaps the AI Giant is disrupting your clients' book accounts, but you can never tell them that.

"What do you reckon, Elle?"

"Possibly, but I won't say anything to anyone. I just think that it's so exciting! I say bring it on! I want to have a go on it, and isn't it great that it is coming into being at the same time as our little monkey?"

They kissed and hugged and had never been happier.

∞

A week after Jim had turned Reaper on for worldwide access, he called another Board Meeting, which included John; Melanie; Bob; and Ivan.

"I have called you here today in order to get any early-bird warning, if there is one. Any problems, Ivan?"

"No, Jim. As you know, Reaper was being used solely by the company's 1.5m employees before you sent it public, now it is being accessed by customers, and would-be customers and Reaper has been handling between 100 million and 120 million searches a day since then. There have been no appreciable problems – only a light slowing in response times, but we are adding extra capacity to alleviate that, and should have fixed it by tomorrow morning".

"Excellent. Melanie?"

"No, only the hardware problem that Ivan just alluded to. We are already onto that one".

"Great. Bob?"

"No, no problems, but it is a little early for law suits. It would normally take a week for one to be drawn up and arrive. Nevertheless, we haven't been informed of any complaints that could possibly lead to legal issues".

"Good. John?"

"No, nothing that hasn't just been mentioned".

"Excellent, excellent. I wanted to get that out of the way before I brought the others in". He pushed a button on the intercom and said, "Will you have the other Board members come in now, please, Marie?"

Emily Smith, the Director of Sales, Keith Roberts, the Director of Advertising, and Jane Davies, Public Relations Manager entered, greeted everyone and took their places.

"Just to bring you guys up to speed', said Jim, "Reaper has been running live with the general public for the last seven days and is handling all customer queries, sales, and, well, just about every interaction. Initial feedback suggests that everything is going extremely well, so I would now like you guys in marketing and sales to sell it, or copies of it. I suggest that you have a chat with John, Bob and Ivan to work out who our most likely customers could be.

"My thoughts are that you could tailor Reaper for car dealerships. Try selling it to Ford, and all the other car manufacturers. Boat and aeroplane manufacturers... and people who book flights, and tourist operators… bus travel companies… anyone who sells tickets – cinema multiplexes… Anyone who deals with large numbers of phone calls or computer enquiries, like call centres… and banks! Bob, could you ask national government, and local, discretely? And the military, Bob!

"Those are a few ideas to be getting on with. Jane, I would like you to keep a steady stream of good news stories appearing in the media: press, TV and online. If you need any storylines, have a chat with John or Ivan. A word of caution though, you cannot mention Ivan by name. Call him 'a team-leader who wishes to remain anonymous'. Remember that, it is vital.

"We haven't worked out prices yet, but basically, if they are worried about cost, they can't afford it. Play on the 'fact' that this new AI software is a game-changer. The time will come when, if you aren't using it in your business, you won't be in business much longer. Mix the fear of being left behind – you know, FOMO - with the pride of being at the pinnacle of technology. Emphasise that My Media is already running on it, and that it can be tailored to suit any business by the very team that developed it for us – the world leaders in Large Language Model AI technology.

"OK, well, I have to dash. I have another appointment, but you can all remain here as long as you like, and if you want drinks or snacks, just ask Marie to order them for you from catering. Don't forget, my door is always open, and my phone is always on. As Project Manager, the same goes for John, I'm sure". John nodded and smiled.

∞

The LLM AI model technology was so new that analysts were stunned at first. Jane Davies was doing a marvellous job of bombarding the media, the news and the tech blogs with up-beat stories on the rosy future the world's population could look forward to when AI was rolled out further. In fact, once Reaper was out, several other AI-lite versions appeared in rapid succession. They were mostly to do with AI image creation, and speech imitation. It soon became possible to create video from sentences; and celebrity voices could be cloned – and were being used in adverts by rogue companies.

There were several cases of blatant misrepresentation, such as that of President Obama selling ice cream using AI generated film and voice over. If it hadn't been too ludicrous to be true, it would have fooled many more people into believing that Obama endorsed Chilly's ice cream in Bali. Later impersonations were more believable, and a fake Jack Nicholson promoting jeans earned the company millions of dollars before it was taken down. The cost of the ad and its placement had been less than $2,ooo.

It was clear that this aspect needed closer regulation, but it did not directly affect Reaper, as Reaper basically only answered questions posed by customers. However, Reaper was a potentially creative tool like some of those that were sprouting up like daisies in spring. Nevertheless, unbeknownst to most people, Jim did have a small company, which was experimenting with AI-driven artwork and narration. He foresaw the uses it could have as a subsidiary of My Media in that he would be able to charge content creators a small sum to have artwork made for their books or album covers, and an even larger sum to narrate their books in a voice of their choosing or even creation.

He was following the Obama and Nicholson cases closely to see how his companies could either follow suit, if the law allowed, or prevent law suits if it didn't. The thought had already crossed his mind that he could move ownership of these artwork companies to countries where cloning famous people was not yet a criminal offence.

∞

There were minor glitches, such as the small number of dispatch depots in which Reaper had tried to process orders for items that had been archived. It had caused a little distress to some people, because they were worried about not getting the refund that they were entitled to, but most customers who experienced this error trusted My Media to reimburse them, so it was not considered a major concern.

There were a few random strange occurrences in ordering, but they were mostly inconsequential and were easily ironed out by checking the coding and giving hefty gift vouchers in compensation. Some content was falsely queried and even marked as of spurious origin.

Despite these annoyances, Jim and his Board judged that all in all, the Reaper out-performed what it had been predicted to be capable of, and so was a great success. Ivan's stature, and that of his team, sky-rocketed within the company, and My Media took the credit in the world outside the Santa Cruz Mountains' depot. That was all right in the beginning, but Ivan sought the recognition that he deserved as the team leader of the greatest innovation in I.T. technology since the Internet had been developed.

The situation was under control at the time, but it could erupt at any moment, mostly because Ivan and the Europeans were illegal immigrants who had been smuggled into the United States by one of it's biggest companies.

The time-bomb was ticking, but no-one had noticed because they were all so flushed with success.

All except Ivan, and the two people who knew him the best, Sonya and Katya.

Ivan attempted to talk to John about the problem. "We need to start making plans about how we are going to tackle the problem of our immigration status, John. As things stand, we could be arrested and deported at any moment".

"We have taken great care to cover our tracks, Ivan. Nobody has the vaguest idea that you are here illegally. My Media has a flawless industrial relations history, so the authorities have no reason to investigate us. Nevertheless, you are right that the situation cannot remain as it is. We have to find a solution soon. I promise that I will talk to Jim about it at the first opportunity that I get".

"Don't procrastinate, John. The press, or one of your competitors could start asking awkward questions about your AI team at any moment. What will you tell them? Do you have anything prepared? No, I thought not. Don't forget who engineered our escape to the West, John. If we are arrested and imprisoned, I will be interrogated, and forced to divulge how we arrived here. Worse still, if we are deported, Putin will not welcome us back with open arms. He is a very vengeful man, John.

"Russia should be getting the accolades for developing the first commercially available LLM AI system, not an American rival industry. We let him down, it will mean a labour camp for us, if we are lucky, and manual labour for our daughters for the rest of their lives. That is, if he doesn't send a hit squad over to assassinate us all. He has been accused of doing that before several times, has he not? Aleksandr Litvinenko and Anna Politkovskaya in 2006. Natalya Estemirova and Sergei Magnitsky in 2009. Boris Nemtsov in 2015. Yevgeny Prigozhin in 2023 and Alexei Navalny in 2024… Did you think we didn't know about these deaths? It is common knowledge all over Russia and the 'Eastern Bloc'…

"If we go down, John, the four top people in My Media will go down too. That is inevitable, no matter how hard you have tried to cover your tracks. Do you remember our conversation about Russian agents in Warsaw? At the very least, the KGB officer in the Warsaw Raffles hotel will be able to identify you, Melanie and Suzanne, and no court in the world will impute that you were not acting on Jim's orders. Had you remembered the agent in the hotel, John? No. I thought not. I did warn you about him or her, didn't I? Do you remember now? It is certain that they will have photos of us together, if not audio too.

"Don't forget to tell Jim that too, will you, John? It is vital that Jim is aware of all the possible outcomes of the situation that he set in motion".

The Bull at the Gate

15: Reaper Flies Like an Eagle

Jim was thoroughly enjoying the acclaim that he was receiving for having produced the first commercially available, and successful, LLM AI model in the world. He had always tended to avoid media publicity, but he had been cornered into giving some short interviews, and thought that he had handled himself rather well. He was more photogenic than he remembered, or maybe he just shined under adulation.

However, there were two questions that kept nagging him. If he controlled the first publicly accessible AI model in the world, what was Brainwave, and who owned it?

It was very unlikely to be a competitor, otherwise they would have brought it to market and be making a fortune like he was. Could he have been interrogating a Russian prototype of Ivan's? It was a possibility, but he doubted that Ivan would admit to it. He had always underplayed Russia's LLM capabilities because he was no longer on the team, although that might have been to increase his perceived value. If he had been in Ivan's position, he would have played it exactly how Ivan had.

Either way, it didn't matter because he was making a fortune out of it, and had already more than doubled his initial investment. Or could it be the Industrial Military Complex? That was most likely. If it were a NATO country, they would have shared their research with the USA anyway, although the US would probably not have been so generous with the other members. It would be renting it to them.

So far, Bob's sales team hadn't received any inquiries from its approaches to the military, which suggested to him that they already had their own version, or were extremely close to it. Their AI needs would not be the same as his commercial version. The military would not need AI that that had been trained to sell books, make book covers and narrate content. He didn't want to get involved with what they would want from AI. It wasn't his business, and he was doing very well without it anyway, although… *Never say never*, he thought.

Ivan and his legal status was the only other real concern that he had, and he was at an impasse. He hadn't yet discussed the matter with Bob. He ought to do it soon, he ought to have done it already – he knew that – but he kept putting it off. He thought about asking Reaper what it 'thought' about his predicament, but again, something, some instinct, was holding him back.

He was worried that Reaper might be bugged.

The National Security Agency at Fort George G. Meade in Maryland was the primary government agency responsible for monitoring and analysing Internet traffic as part of its broader mandate to ensure national security. That was no longer a secret after the Edward Snowden disclosures in 2013. Furthermore, the NSA's surveillance activities often involved collaboration with other agencies, such as the Federal Bureau of Investigation and programs like PRISM.

Although, the NSA's focus was supposed to be on foreign intelligence, its operations overlapped with domestic surveillance. How much attention were they paying to Reaper? If they were monitoring Reaper closely in order to better understand it, and possibly clone its most advanced features, surely they would notice if he started asking questions about illegal Russian immigrant scientists?

After all, the Russian government had been complaining about the disappearance or possible abduction of Ivan and his team, although they weren't mentioned by name, so if he started making reverse image inquiries, surely it wouldn't take the NSA long to link the two, and be knocking on his door.

He wondered whether he could make the inquiries from a different country by using VPN. Perhaps, he could make it look as if the inquiries were coming from Iran, but dismissed that because he was sure that VPN would not fool the NSA, and why would a foreign power be inquiring about getting American citizenship for émigré Russian scientists?

No, Bob was his only route, and he would be furious that he had not been consulted from the very beginning, and Jim couldn't blame him for thinking that. It was a total mess, but it had made him a great deal of money.

"Marie? Can you get hold of Robert Saunders, legal, for me, please, and set up a meeting for tomorrow morning? Thank you".

∞

"I have called this meeting together for the purposes of assessing sales of Reaper, and where we can go from here. I'd also like to know where the competition is and what it is doing. Is there anything that we should be doing to maintain our competitive edge, if in fact we are still the world leaders… and if we're not, why aren't we?". Jim expected a small laugh from the limited Board and got one.

"OK, where shall we start? Emily! Sales?"

"Thank you. Our department consulted with Ivan about his views on the commercial capabilities of Reaper, and how he saw those capabilities expanding. We had representatives from Keith's department – advertising – and Bob's legal department present too. Ivan explained that Reaper has been designed to perform specific tasks that typically require human intelligence, such as: language processing; pattern recognition; decision-making, and problem-solving.

"Armed with this knowledge, we sought out companies and organisations that focus on voiced assistance, like Siri, and Alexa; personalised recommendations, like Netflix and Spotify; image and speech recognition, such as, photo tagging and transcription, like social media.

"Future areas of expansion could be healthcare diagnostics, that is identifying diseases; finance algorithms for use in fraud detection; and autonomous driving technology for use in driverless taxis and automated delivery services for things like pizzas and home shopping. John will be able to tell you more about those developments.

"So, we have been specifically targetting places like call centres and organisations that employ staff in customer service rôles, data entry and routine administrative jobs, and we have had some success. We are currently running phased trials with four of the top five international call centres, namely: ConnectSphere Solutions; EchoLink Support; PulsePoint Contact Services, and VoiceBridge International. The fifth largest, ChatStream Dynamics, is interested but wants to carry out more independent research first.

"The four that are with us, albeit tentatively, have more that one million employees. Initial studies have shown that in call centres where emotional empathy is not normally required, Reaper can replace 70% of staff".

Emily looked around the table to judge reactions. Most were astounded.

"Pricing has always been difficult because Reaper is unique - the first of its kind - but if a call centre has 100,000 employees worldwide, and pays an average salary of, say, $10,000 a year, that would mean a saving of $700,000,000 per annum! We could easily ask for $500,000,000 and arrange for maintenance and support. And, let me remind you that when

I say, $700 million, I am only talking about one-tenth – 10% - of the staff at the four biggest call centres. If we win these contracts, we will be taking $7 billion annually from this segment alone… and there are literally thousands of smaller call centres!

"We are charging 20% of our 'normal fee' for these trials, which we have contracted to carry out for four months, so we are earning approximately $167 million over the trial periods.

"We also have trials with the top film and music rental companies, and are earning similar amounts there too. I have submitted the exact figures through the proper channels".

"Thank you, Emily. John how is the image recognition aspect of Reaper coming along?"

"Despite it being the last AI feature of Reaper to be developed, we are the world leader in image recognition software – Emily, the police may be interested in this for use in spotting known criminals in crowds – image creation too… and video from sentences or words, as we call it. We are currently working with local hospitals to train Reaper to spot various diseases by the use of archive hospital footage from real cases.

"We haven't tested Reaper on live patients yet, because the hospital's legal department need more assurances. I think it's fair to say that Bob, in our own team, feels that that is the best way to go too. Let us prove to the hospitals that Reaper is accurate, and then let them call us to install it for trials. It shifts the burden of responsibility a little more fairly towards the hospitals.

"In any case, the big picture is very promising. We have had zero cases of misdiagnosis so far even in complicated cancer cases where surgeons have to take the utmost care, because the visual picture of the cancer is either unclear, or it resembles another disease".

"Keith – advertising? Yes, sir. We have been targeting the types of companies that Ivan identified and that Emily and John have alluded to. We are also seeking out other firms and other industries which could use Reaper to save money, such as those sectors identified on the hand-out you gave us from Brainwave. I have made a note about law enforcement, John. Thank you. If we don't get a response, we initiate a follow-up sequence until we get a soft 'Yes' or 'No'. We are also working with Jane on public relations and press releases. I'm sure everyone has seen pieces in the media. Nobody, not even a senator's fund-raising team, could be making more phone calls than we are".

"And, last but not least, our Director of Talent Management, Suzanne. Tell us what has been happening in our own little company".

"Yes, thank you. As you are probably aware, My Media employs about 1.5 million staff worldwide. About 500,000 are involved with call centre duties. About 65% of these are based in the US, and their average salary is not $10,000 per annum, but $30,000, So, we spend about $10 billion annually on call centre staff" She paused for effect. "$10 billion annually. We have been running internal trials, and we too reckon that we could shed about 70% of these staff.

"Of course, employment laws are tougher in the US than in many countries – certainly outside Europe. We will need to retrain the better staff, but we will still no longer require hundreds of thousands of our existing employees. Last year, our chairman had the foresight to implement the renewal of expiring employment contracts for six months only, so we have started to shed employees through natural wastage, but we could make scheduled redundancies, and offer voluntary redundancies to trim our workforce, thereby increasing savings more quickly".

"I imagine that that will have to be carried out in conjunction with Bob of legal".

"So, there you have the global picture", said Jim. "Three months after the introduction of AI to the world, the world is pleased with AI and Reaper, in my view. Reaper handles calls and queries quickly and accurately – very accurately- and from an employer's perspective is always on call. No more pandemic problems! No more sick notes… We will always need human call centre operatives – well, for the foreseeable future anyway – because Reaper is not able to empathise, it had no emotions, and some people are very emotional… often unnecessarily so, but there you have it. Reaper has proved to be the best investment that My Media has ever made with the exception of a few key personnel.

"Thank you, ladies and gentlemen. Bob have you got a moment, please? In my office".

Jim went to the bar in his office, and took two large tins of Guinness from the fridge, and two pint glasses. He knew what Bob's favourite tipple was.

"Here, Bob. Have you had time to reflect on that little matter I told you about?"

"Little matter? Cheers! This ain't no little matter, Jim". Bob was allowed to call him by the diminutive of his first name. "I wish you had brought me in earlier".

"You would have advised against it, and there would be no Reaper…"

"Possibly, but then, you wouldn't be facing jail either".

"I'm not facing jail…"

"No, not yet, but only because you haven't been found out yet! Tell me the whole story. Right from the beginning. How did you get yourself into this situation".

Jim told Bob the whole story leaving nothing out.

"OK, well, thanks for that. Let me go away, have a few more Guinnesses and think about it. In the meantime, keep everyone sweet, and keep doing whatever it is you have been doing so far. I'll call you soon".

Jim felt better after having unburdened himself onto his trusted friend. Bob would know what to do – he always did – even though sometimes Bob's solutions were unpleasant".

∞

"When are they going to sort out our citizenship, Ivan?" asked Sonya. "We've been in America for nine months already, and the only place we've seen is Macy's! You have made My Media billions of dollars, and they have made us prisoners! I don't know how much longer the kids and I can take it! The three of us see only the three of us, and your European team, and that's all the people we have met for nine months. It's not fair on the children. They haven't got any friends…

"When are you going to stand up for them, and me, and the rest of us?" His wife's sobs, and obvious distress saddened him greatly.

"We may seem to be prisoners, but we are very wealthy. Wealthy far beyond our wildest dreams, and our prison is the best place we have ever lived in, my dear. I believe that Jim is doing all he can. I mean, this is a very busy time for him and the Reaper team. We need to sell Reaper while we still have a virtual monopoly on this AI model. Our competition is catching up fast. When they bring their products to the market, the prices will drop, and the dash will be over…"

"How rich do you want to be? How happy do you want your family to be, Ivan? Those are the questions"

He hugged her to him, but she resisted. "Jim could send us back to the labour camps any time he wanted to, Ivan. You do realise that, don't you? What will happen when he doesn't need you any more? I bet he's already got you training up Americans who could take over from you. Has he?"

"It is only common sense to do that, my dear. If I died, the project must go on…"

"If you die? What are you going to die of? You're 46 years old! A road accident? We don't go anywhere! A heart attack? Are you willing to work so hard for a billionaire that you die of a heart attack in your forties and leave your children fatherless? Do you think that Jim would consider doing that for you for even five seconds? No! Of course not! He is not as stupid as you!

"If you die, what use is a widow and two teenage girls to him? None at all. We'll be a burden. He could leave us here to rot, or turn us in as illegal immigrants – or have us turned in! That's more his style…" He tried to comfort her again.

"It's all right for you, you're working with hundreds of clever people every day. You have your work and excitement in your life. What have we got? Each other and the television… It's not enough, Ivan, it's just not enough. We need some stimulation too…" She looked into his eyes.

"I promise that I will talk with John again next time I see him, and if I get nowhere with him, I will speak directly to Jim. I know how hard it is on you and the girls, my dear, but it won't be for much longer, I promise". Ivan was genuinely affected by his wife's fears, but he was already thinking about how to implement an upgrade to Reaper without having to turn it off for an hour.

16: Reaper Rolls Out Worldwide

"I call this meeting to order".

"Thank you, George. Emily, sales, please", said Jim

"Thank you", she had a huge smile on her face. "New Trials. We have entered into trial periods with all five of the major hotel chains in the world! They are: Summit Lodging International ; Horizon Hospitality Group; GlobalStay Resorts & Suites; Vista Hotels Worldwide; Unity Inn & Resorts. This is a major coup. Let me run some figures past you.

"Summit Lodging International has over 1.5 million rooms across 8,600+ properties. It handles millions of bookings annually. Its workforce is estimated at over 400,000 employees worldwide.

"Horizon Hospitality Group has more than 1.1 million rooms across 7,000+ properties. It employs approximately 430,000 people globally

"GlobalStay Resorts & Suites or GSR&S has nearly 6,000 properties and manages over 700,000 rooms. Its global workforce numbers around 350,000 employees, including those at franchised and directly managed properties.

"Vista Hotels Worldwide operates approximately 9,200 properties with over 828,000 rooms globally. Its employee count is estimated to be about 170,000, primarily in franchise and customer-facing rôles.

"Unity Inn & Resorts with a portfolio of 5,400+ hotels and around 821,000 rooms, UI&R employs approximately 250,000 people globally, across various functions such as front-desk operations, maintenance, and management.

I have done the maths for you, so that is 1.6 million employees, handling 4.12 million rooms in 36,200 properties worldwide. We are still working on how many staff Reaper can replace. It won't be as high as in the call centres, because of catering and cleaning staff, but a rough estimate could be that approximately 40-50% would be affected by deploying Reaper, so minimum 800,000 people at a global average of about $10 per hour, therefore the global saving could be $8 million per hour, at least half of which will accrue to Reaper.

"Yes, $8 million per hour twenty-four / seven... A massive $70 billion annually.

"Smaller chains are also interested, and we are likely to achieve similar results. Depending on our depth of penetration of this market, we could easily double or even triple that amount.

"The trials with the call centres are almost at an end, and every single trial company is going to take up Reaper! The fifth chain of call centres has seen which way the wind is blowing, and has booked a consultation. The hospital trials are also near completion. I am pleased to announce that Reaper is now diagnosing certain diseases faster and more accurately than most human doctors. They will be taking it up, and when they roll it out across their network of hospitals, then others will follow suit. The rewards will be even larger in the medical field, because obviously medical staff earn way more that call centre staff.

"In fact, the top five hospital chains in the USA alone own 760 hospitals, which employ at least 100,000 medical staff that could face replacement by Reaper. These figures are very tentative… it could be three or even four times more, let's say 100,000 staff – only in the top five chains, I remind you – each earning roughly \$70k per annum – is \$7 billion dollars.

"Those top hospital chains employ only about 20% of the country's medical diagnosticians, so we are talking about \$35 billion annually.

And finally, the top five car dealerships employ about 100,000 staff on an average salary of about \$60,000. Say that Reaper could affect half of those jobs, then we are talking about \$3 billion annually.

"A complete list of where he have penetrated and to what extent is on my handout in front of you".

When Emily sat down there was a stunned silence at the table. Not even Jim had foreseen the enormity of the potential earnings from Reaper, and at the moment they were concentrating on rolling it out to only the top five companies in every sector of industry. They hadn't yet even begun to think of how to sell it, or probably rent it out to the public on subscription. How many hundreds of millions of individuals would pay $20 per month for access to a cut-down Reaper, and how many companies, especially, in the media, would pay $100-$500 per month for a more powerful version?

"So much was yet unknown. They were in unchartered territory. They only knew that they had to plough on, before the opposition caught up with them.

When the meeting was over, Jim sat in his office alone thinking about all that money. It would surely make him the richest kid on the block now.

It was his wife's sixtieth birthday the following week, and the girls were coming home for it. He would have to do something very special for them, but it was not his field at all. He had always avoided going to and throwing parties when it was at all possible. He'd do what he done for the last decade, and call the firm's catering department in to organise it for him, and he'd go into town to get her some expensive jewellery. He'd get the kids something too.

"Sir, I have Ivan Ivanovich outside. He'd like to have a word if you have a few minutes".

"Yes, Marie. Send him in".

"Hello, Ivan, what can I do for you. Let's sit at the coffee table. A cold beer and a vodka? Good man. I'll join you. Cheers!"

"Na zdorovye!"

"Yes, na zdorovye! Wow! That hits the spot. I'm glad you turned me on to this Moskovskaya. It's better that what I used to serve up. Now, what can I do for you? A problem with Reaper?"

"No. Nothing like that. I can handle Reaper. What is bothering me is much more difficult to handle. My wife, Sonya, and the children are unhappy. They feel cooped up, as if they are in prison. Sonya complains that they never meet anyone. In short, she wants American citizenship for all of us so that we can come and go as we please. Go into town, and take a weekend away whenever work permits".

"Ah, I see. Well, I'm glad that you have brought this up, Ivan. John has mentioned it several times, and I have asked Bob for his advice. Why, I was talking to him only last week about it. He is due to get back to me any time soon. I'll give him a ring right now, if you like.

"Hi, Bob. Look. I've got Ivan with me, and he and his family are concerned about what we discussed a few times. You know… Yes, that's right. I don't want to talk about it over the phone, but how are you getting on with it? … OK, well, we'll leave it at that for now… Yes, I'll tell him. Bye".

"Let me top you up. Bob says that he has several ideas, but he is not sure which is the best yet. He'll pop in and let me know in a few days, then I, or he, can explain it to you. Is that all right?"

"It is for me, Jim, but I can't guarantee that it will be enough for Sonya. As far as she is concerned, she has been waiting for citizenship for more than nine months, and that is a long time to have one's movement restricted – ten times worse than when Covid-19 struck, as she keeps saying".

"Yes. I understand, but we have been so busy with Reaper… I'm sure that you understand…"

"Yes, Jim. I understand perfectly, and so does Sonya deep down, but she is coming to the end of her tether".

"OK, I'll tell you what. It is my wife's sixtieth birthday next Friday. I'm going to put on a garden party for her over at our place… in the afternoon. A marquee, food, drinks, some music. Why don't you bring your wife and daughters… and the whole team? My daughters will be there too. How old are yours? Oh, eleven and thirteen… mine are… um, in their thirties, but I'm sure they'll get along.

"At least it'll get Sonya out of this place, and she can meet people. I'm sure that it must be difficult for an intelligent woman like Sonya to be so confined for so long. You can tell her that Bob is onto your citizenship problem personally too… and so am I! Make sure she knows that the top people in the firm are doing their very best to help – not just lower staff!"

"OK, Jim. Thank you. It does raise one more question though".

"Yes? We are going to have to go into town again to get Mrs. Diamond a present, and new outfits for the women".

Jim smiled, but he was thinking, *No matter what you try to do, there's always something!*

∞

When he got home that evening, Jim told his wife about the birthday party that he had in mind. He couldn't keep it a secret, because of all the staff coming and going, but he didn't tell her about the diamond tiara he was thinking of getting her. He had never seen her wear one, and hoped that it was something she'd like.

"What do you think, Marion?"

"Sixty all ready! I don't really want anyone to know, if I'm honest…"

"You don't look a day over thirty-five!" he said kissing her hand. It was true that she had spent a fortune on her looks, especially in the last two decades, but she exercised regularly and was always following one fad diet or another to the frustration of her personal trainer and dietician.

"Thank you, darling. You always say the sweetest things. Do I really look thirty-five? I hope so, but it is getting harder and harder every year to keep looking this way…" She was looking at her profiles in the reflective glass of one of the cabinets nearby.

"We can afford whatever you want, Marion. You just stay happy".

"In that case, I'm looking forward to my party. You know the girls will be here. They always loved a good party. Be sure to tell them about it in case they want to invite some school friends, or get in some special food or music".

"OK, my darling". He had noticed that she was becoming slightly more childlike, and more forgetful as she got older, and hoped that it wasn't Alzheimer's. He kissed her hand again. "I'd better get some work done".

"Oh, do you have to? Just sit with me for half an hour, and we'll watch the news together like we did in the old days", by which she meant before they had become millionaires.

"Of course. That would be nice. Just like in the good old days when there were enough hours in the day". Marion looked at him quizzically and then at the giant TV on the wall opposite as Jim clicked it on.

The item was part way through, but they caught that rioting in Shanghai was being vigorously put down by the authorities. Six had been shot dead, dozens wounded and hundreds corralled into the local football stadium under arrest. There followed an item on public demonstrations in Bengaluru, Mumbai, and Hyderabad in India.

"Do you really want to watch this stuff, Marion. It's so depressing. The world has never had it so good, but people never stop complaining. He turned the sound down to inaudible. If those young people knew what awful lives their grandparents, and even their parents had had to endure, they'd be more grateful to capitalism and world leaders for dragging them out of poverty. Jesus wept! Did you see the background to the rioters in the footage on China? I've seen parts of American cities that look worse than that... Los

Angeles, San Francisco, New York! What have they got to complain about. Sixty years ago, Chairman bloody Mao was slaughtering their grandparents, and twenty years ago millions of them were in forced labour camps. You'd never guess it now, but still they're complaining.

"Sorry, Marion. It makes my blood boil. Why do you want to watch that kind of stuff?"

"I don't, my dear, I just want to be with you and talk sometimes… I get very lonely, you know… I miss the days when we used to go on family picnics, or all play Monopoly together. They were such happy times, weren't they?" He kissed her forehead and squeezed her tight.

"Yes, darling, they were very happy days. You have made me the happiest, and luckiest man alive. I know I get too wrapped up in the business, but I never stop thinking of you, darling, and there has never been anyone else…"

"No, I believe you. I just miss you… and the girls… It'll be lovely for us all to be home together again, after the party is over…" and she began to sing the refrain quietly. Jim joined in with her singing one of her favourite songs by Joni James:

"The party's over, it's time to call it a day…
They burst your pretty balloon,
And taken the moon away…
It's time to wind up the masquerade,
Just make your mind up, the piper must be paid.
The party's over…"

Hard man though he thought he was, the tears trickled down his cheeks, as he watched the muted TV in disgust, although the topic had changed to one on floods in the UK. He wasn't weeping for the victims on the TV though, he missed those olden days too.

For the first time that he could remember in a very long time, he sat holding his wife on the sofa, and thought that work could go hang for the rest of the day. He was going to enjoy his wife's company in front of a mock open fire, because it was warm enough, and a muted TV showing worldwide disasters.

He switched to the rental channel of My Media, and chose the film 'Singing In The Rain' with Gene Kelly. It was one of their joint favourites from 'The Good Old Days'. When it started, Marion opened her eyes, recognising it immediately. "Are we going to watch it together?"

"You betcha, gal!" said Jim. Marion giggled and snuggled up closer to him as they sang along to all the old classic songs. It was the first time they had done this for decades, and they were enjoying it.

17: Wheel-Wobble

"Thank you, Emily. You and your sales team are going from strength to strength. Everybody has done, and continues to do, a great job. I will admit that I had not foreseen how important to world commerce Reaper would become. There will be big bonuses this year throughout the company's staff worldwide, and you can pass that on to staff at all levels in the company. Let them know that I appreciate their – your – hard work and dedication to the Reaper Project. I applaud you all!", and he clapped his hands three times to demonstrate it.

"May I say something?" asked Suzanne. "Certainly. By all means. What is it, Suzanne?"

"Well. This is difficult after all the good news. I don't want to be the one to burst anyone's bubble, but Reaper is having a huge effect on the global job market…"

"In certain fields", said Emily. "When viewed as a whole, Reaper is not affecting low-end manual labour, which accounts for the vast majority of work in Third World Countries…"

"You can say that, Emily, but research shows that Reaper and its successors, because, like it or not, other companies are starting to bring their own models on stream now, Reaper et al are expected to have a significant impact on a large portion of the global labour market. Sure, certain sectors are less likely to be disrupted, such as farm labour, as you rightly point out. Sectors such as agriculture, which require hands-on, physical labour and local knowledge, may see much lower exposure to automation, especially for lower-skill positions. For example, in emerging markets, where agriculture remains a dominant sector, AI's immediate influence may be around 26%, suggesting that manual or farm labour jobs are less likely to be automated in the short term compared to office-based or technical jobs

"However, global projections suggest that AI may affect up to 40% of global jobs, with advanced economies experiencing higher levels of impact, particularly in routine or high-skill rôles. This suggests that AI will affect cities the most, because cities house office blocks. So, what will happen if 40% of the workforce of a city loses its job? What would happen if 40% of the population of San Francisco lost its job?

"Think about it? Mass unemployment, empty office block, desolate city centres!"

"Yes, excuse me, Suzanne, but what has this got to do with My Media?" asked Jim. "We are providing a tool that other companies can use, if they choose to buy it, in order to streamline their companies. That is their Board's decision, and nothing to do with us. Let the government retrain the unemployed… let the government alter the school curriculum to suit the New World Order that is coming to pass – that's what we pay our taxes for. It sounds as if you're suggesting that we halt the advance of technology in order to preserve the status quo. That's Ludditism… sabotage – throw a spanner in the works… What I would like to know is, how is Reaper affecting our workforce, and what are we doing to mitigate the effects of Reaper? Tell me that story, but don't ask me to fix the problems of the world because we happened to highlight them with our recent innovation.

"Permit me just to say this, before I let you carry on. Reaper has exposed sloth, and tired old-fashioned ways of working. Just like in the earlier half of the 20th century when computers changed the old ways of office working! Previously, there had been vast rooms with hundreds of clerks using adding machines and typewriters – clack, clack, clackity, clack, clack. Computers changed all that making millions of middle-class workers redundant. They retrained and retired, and office work became streamlined. It did away with all those boring , mind-numbing jobs, and schools raised their sights. Pupils were taught more. Resulting in more kids needing to go to university. Society benefitted from the computer revolution! Likewise when the Internet evolved. The same will happen with Reaper.

"Society will retrain, or retire. The workforce will get better jobs, and the human race will move another step forward. So, please... We cannot change the world, and I for one, will not stand in the way of progress. Besides, if it hadn't been us, it would have been someone else. Jesus wept! Even the Russians were more advanced than we were! They would have had no compunction about rolling it out and upsetting middle-class office workers, would they?

"Anyway, please continue".

"Yes. Well, as predicted, Reaper has affected about 70% of our workforce – er, 71.2% to be precise. This represents 1,068,000 workers. We began renewing expiring contracts with six-month contracts last year, and, coupled with natural wastage, we have managed to shed 31% of that number, so, 331,080 without any significant problems. We now need to decide what to do about the remaining 736,920 workers. I suggest a programme of voluntary redundancy suited to local wage scales, and an in-house retraining programme where possible".

"Yes", said Jim, "I agree. We don't want any come-back on us. If what you say is true about the effect Reaper is having on the global labour market, we need to be able to point to how we have not contributed to the problem, because we have done the right thing by our workforce. Do you see what I mean? When the proverbial hits the fan, and the unions or whatever start blaming us, we will be able to say, 'Our workers aren't complaining, because we treated them fairly. It's not our fault that other companies didn't do the same'. And it's true! It is not our fault.

"I like the idea of in-house re-training, but only to fill vacancies that we require. We could also make a donation to the local government Labour Exchanges abroad to help them find jobs for the wave of unemployed… Or better still, we could set up a network of agencies to provide labour to local industries – like Manpower – what are they called now… employment agencies or talent acquisition firms. Yes, we could set up our own global network of talent acquisition firms.

"Bob, can you get someone to look into that? Great! Anyone for any more? No? Then I declare this meeting closed".

Suzanne stayed close to John, and when Jim had left the room, she said, "John, can we have a word, please?"

"Sure, do you want to come to my office now?"

Once seated at his coffee table, and tea and biscuits had been brought in, John looked enquiringly at Suzanne. "Have you been following the news?" she said.

"I don't get a lot of chance these days, but I try to keep up. What's bothering you specifically?"

"The riots worldwide about job losses due to AI – and especially Reaper!"

Oh, well, I tend to agree with Jim. My Media is doing right by its employees. And if other companies don't, well, that's not our fault…"

"That's the easy way out, yes, and it's technically correct, yes, but we still have to live in this world. As you know, not all news gets to be reported in the media, so I sent out a global request to all our depot managers in the world asking for info on local demonstrations, riots and the like. Listen to this". She removed a sheet of paper from her briefcase and read

"Major rioting in all regions with well-established Business Process Outsourcing, or BPO, industries. In particular:

1] The Philippines:

> • Metro Manila: Home to about 80% of the country's call centres. Rioting and looting. Troops on the streets. Gunfire; some dead.

> • Cebu City: A major hub for technical support and customer service. Rioting and looting. Troops on the streets. Baton charges; nearby hospitals full to capacity.

> • Davao City, Bacolod, Iloilo, and Baguio: These cities also have significant BPO operations. Rioting and looting. Troops on the streets. Gunfire, but no wounded reported.

2] India:

> • Bangalore: Known as the Silicon Valley of India, it supports numerous I.T.-enabled services. Demonstrations. Police baton charges.

- Hyderabad: A hub for tech and customer support. Demonstrations.
- Mumbai and Delhi NCR (Gurgaon and Noida): Important for diverse BPO operations. Rioting and looting. Troops on the streets.

3] Malaysia:

- Kuala Lumpur: Central location for multilingual call centres supporting global clients. Demonstrations outside government offices. Police wielding batons on the streets in riot gear.

3] China:

- Shanghai and Beijing: Major hubs for multilingual and technical support services. Demonstrations. Armed police in riot gear.

4] Vietnam:

- Ho Chi Minh City: Emerging as a growing BPO destination due to its cost efficiency and skilled workforce. Demonstrations. Armed police on the streets in riot gear.

"These call centres collectively employ millions of workers, providing support for industries ranging from technology to finance and hospitality. For instance, the Philippines alone employs over 1.4 million people in its BPO sector.

"The list goes on and on… the UK, the EU, South America, South Africa; Mexico, Canada… John, you might be thinking, sure but it won't happen here, but you'd be wrong. My findings continue:

In the United States, the largest call centres are predominantly located in major metro areas with access to a large labour pool. Key locations include:

1.	Phoenix, Arizona: Hosts significant operations for companies like American Express and Bank of America, with thousands of employees each. Demonstrations and graffiti. State police.

2.	Dallas, Texas Area: Cities like Irving and Richardson house operations for Citibank and Blue Cross Blue Shield. Rioting; National Guard.

3.	Jacksonville, Florida: Home to Florida Blue and Citigroup facilities, each employing thousands. Spontaneous demonstrations; National Guard.

4.	San Antonio, Texas: Another hub for Citigroup operations. Large demonstrations; State police.

5.	Tampa, Florida: A location for Citigroup's extensive call center workforce. Widespread unrest; National Guard.

6.	Sioux Falls, South Dakota: Hosts Wells Fargo and Citibank facilities. Demonstrations, graffiti.

7.	Westlake, Texas: A center for Fidelity Investments. Demonstrations.

8.	Greensboro, North Carolina: UnitedHealth Group operates a large call center here. Unruly demonstrations, vandalism; State police

9.	Norfolk, Virginia: Bank of America has a significant call center presence. Spontaneous demonstrations, rioting, vandalism, graffiti; National Guard.

"John, these centres employ thousands of workers, often exceeding 2,000 staff per site, depending on the company and the services provided. Did you get that, John? *'In the United States, the largest call centres are predominantly located in major metro areas with access to a large labour pool'.* Do you realise what that means? If you sack 70% of people where there is 'a large labour pool' – it is going to be darned difficult to impossible for them to find another job! Will that mean mass migration? Migration to where? Mass poverty? Massive civil unrest? Revolution?"

"There have already been demonstrations of thousands and thousands of people in all these American cities, but they are not getting any air time, because the government is saying the same as Jim. It's not their problem.

"It doesn't stop there though, there have been isolated incidents in hundreds of larger towns and cities. Smashed windows, graffiti, acts of vandalism all on the increase all over the country!

"Why even here in Silicon Valley, hundreds of medical staff have written letters to the Chief Administrative Officer of Sierra Valley Health Institute in San Jose protesting about the possible use of AI in medical diagnostics and the subsequent expected loss of jobs. My sister told me that. She's a doctor there. Did it see on the news? No! These are upper middle-class workers who wouldn't usually say boo to a goose!

"Believe me, John, it's getting bad out there… and the answer from people like Jim is, 'It's not my fault. It's none of my business. Let them retrain, or let them find another job, or it'll all sort itself out in a few years…

"What are those people expected to do for a few years while it all sorts itself out, John? Do you want to live in smashed, looted cities that are unsafe to walk in? Because that's where we're heading to!"

John looked concerned, but more for his friend's mental health. He didn't believe that there was significant civil unrest in America. How could there be? He would have heard about it, surely?

"Well, Su. I don't know what to say. I haven't seen the things you're talking about. Don't get me wrong, I believe you – I really do… I mean, you have done your research, and your sister told you about the letters, but I can't understand why it hasn't been on TV, or none of my friends have said anything to me".

"Who's going to tell big John Dickenson that there are riots and demonstrations on the streets of all major US cities, eh? They would expect you to know, and the fact that you don't talk about it, just proves to them that you don't care. People misidentify your ignorance as apathy or indifference. As Rome burns, you swan about in your ivory tower up in the Santa Cruz Mountains lording it over the Reaper Project! The very project that is ruining the lives of millions of people at your feet!"

"Come on now, that's a bit strong, isn't it? I mean, casting me as nutty Nero fiddling while the workers of the world set the planet on fire? Don't you think you're over-reacting my friend? Let's have a brandy, shall we?"

Suzanne nodded, but knew she was closer to the truth than John was.

18: The Celebrations

Jim and Marion hired a helicopter taxi to get them to Norman Y. Mineta San Jose International Airport to meet their daughters who were flying in together from New York.

"What are all those people doing down there, Jim?"

"Oh, it's just a bunch of lay-about students protesting about something they don't know anything about, I suppose. Students have been doing it since Vietnam. Everybody's sick to death of them". Marion nodded, believed him, and concentrated on seeing the kids for the first time that year.

"Oh, I'm so looking forward to seeing little Gail and Jeannie again!" she said with a smile from one ear to the other.

"They're in their thirties…" he said, and wished he hadn't said anything to burst her bubble. "Won't be long now". When they flew into the airport, they descended over the heads of a group of about a hundred protestors. Jim read one of the placards, "People want humans at Air Traffic Control, not robots!'

They were back home with their children forty-five minutes later. "Did you see all those people?" asked Marion of her daughters, "Were any of them school friends?"

The girls looked at each other and shrugged.

"I didn't recognise anyone, Mom. It's the same in New York and San Francisco…" said Jeannie.

"It's the same all over America!" said Gail.

"It's the same all over the world, Mom" they said together and laughed. "Don't you watch the news any more?" asked Jeannie.

"Or read the newspapers?" asked Gail.

"No, not any more. Your father doesn't approve. It's all bad news. We don't want a lot of bad news at our age…"

"If Dad doesn't want to watch the news, then that's up to him!" said Jeannie, "but if you want to watch it, that's up to you. It's none of his business".

"Women need to stick up for their rights, Mom… especially the more senior ladies. Young women wouldn't stand for it any more…"

"Gail's right. If you want to watch the news, you bloody well watch the news, Mom!"

"No profanity, please, darling. Oh, your father's right. Why depress ourselves on purpose? They never say anything nice. Let's go out to the pool. It's cooler by the water. I'll have Marie bring us out some lemonade and sandwiches, or would you prefer a glass of milk and some biscuits?"

"To be honest, I'd prefer a beer, Mom" said Jeannie.

"Me too", said Gail.

"Tut, tut. Where did we go wrong? You shouldn't be drinking alcohol at your ages". The sisters looked at each other and shrugged again. They hadn't had the courage to tell their mother that all their friends were blaming their father for ruining the job market globally and causing mass unrest on the streets of almost every city in the world.

Not yet, anyway.

∞

Guests started to arrive at one o'clock by all manner of cars, limousines, motorcycles and helicopter. The Diamonds were in the grounds waiting for them. Each of the four of them had chosen some of their friends, although Marion had drawn up the main guest list, and Jim had chosen a few select colleagues from My Media. Ivan and his friends, Eduard, Alex and Katya, John, and Bob from the legal department. Gail and Jeannie had invited a few old school and college friends, and Marion had invited dozens of friends from her charities, and her bridge club.

During the mid afternoon, at the height of the festivities, a rumble could be heard from outside the grounds. It was obvious that all of the guests could hear it, because they could be seen turning to look in the direction of where the noise was coming from, although the perimeter wall and the gates could not be seen from where they were because of the landscaping. A house security guard approached Jim.

"Sir, there's a disturbance at the front gate. Some sort of demonstration. What do you want me to do about it?"

"Disperse it, man! Send them packing".

"I don't have the authority, sir. They're not actually trespassing on your property".

"They are on our private road, Bill! Get them off it!"

"Sir, it is a private road, but it is also a public thoroughfare. If they had arrived by vehicle, I could move them on, but they walked here, and they have the right to do that".

"Do they have the right to cause a public nuisance of themselves? What about Disturbing the Peace? Or Harassment or Intimidation? Or Public Nuisance? There must be something we can do. Ask Mr. Robert Saunders if I can speak to him". The guard walked off to look for Bob, but he couldn't help thinking that his boss had seemed to be getting overly riled by such a trifling demonstration, which could cause no-one any harm. It was so unlike the usually unflappable Jim Diamond.

When Bob arrived minutes later, he said, "We don't want to be seen to be cracking a nut with a sledgehammer, Jim. Our worldwide image has already taken quite a hammering recently. Sorry, no pun intended. Have you seen the share price? It's down 20% Let me phone the police department. I'll see if they can invoke Disturbing the Peace under the California Penal Code § 415. In the meantime, try to calm down. There's no sense in having a heart attack over a few demonstrators". Bob walked a few paces off.

"Well, I spoke to the Chief of Police at the PAPD. He didn't really want to get involved. He said it was because that's a private road, but my guess is that the real reason is he's worried about deselection because of all the civil unrest so far this year, and he doesn't want to be seen sticking up for such an unpopular entity as My Media, which has become synonymous with Reaper, which has a very bad press worldwide. He's going to send a couple of squad cars around though.

"I'm afraid that unless things escalate, there's not much more that we can do right now. Why not aim a couple of loudspeakers at the gate and turn the volume up".

"Like the CIA did with Noriega in the embassy, you mean?"

"Manuel Noriega and Operation Just Cause in 1989? Heavens, no. I just meant to cancel the din that the protesters are making. Lighten up, Jim. Have a drink with your family – you don't all get together often. I'll sort the speakers out and give the guard at the gate my cell phone number in case the police want to speak to someone. Go on. I've got this…"

Jim tapped his friend's shoulder, nodded and walked off. Bob smiled and shook his head slightly, feeling sorry for his old friend. It was obvious that the world unrest was getting to him, although he pretended that it had nothing to do with him. He walked down to the gatehouse to pass on his phone number and reconnoitre the scene for himself. He estimated the number of protesters to be about 200, and they were fairly peaceful, but loud.

"Hi, er, Paul", he said reading the guard's name tag. "Any problems? I'm Bob Saunders of the My Media legal department". They shook hands.

"No, Mr Saunders. Nothing we can't handle". He was referring to himself, his dog, the house security staff of two, and a few gardeners.

"Good. Keep it legal, eh? You stay this side of the gate, and they stay that side. The police are on their way, but they didn't sound enthusiastic about getting involved, so don't expect much help from them. If you need me for anything, here's my card. My cell is on it. Keep up the good work. Er, Paul, it wouldn't hurt if you discretely filmed the protesters. You never know, if it went to court, it might be useful to have some mug shots. Try not to get any voices though. We can't use recorded voice without both parties' permission in the State of California, though we could have the audio track removed if we had to. I suppose".

Bob walked back to the party to talk with the sound engineer about shuffling the loudspeakers about, then he had to speak with Ivan.

"Ivan, great party, eh? Are you and Sonya enjoying yourselves? Ivan, do you have a few minutes? I want a word in private. I promise that I won't keep your husband long, Sonya. Let's take a walk around Jim's magnificent grounds, Ivan. They really are a delight. I have had a couple of ideas about your citizenship. I have run them past Jim already, and he pretty much told me to let you pick which way you want to go. There's no rush. Discuss it with your friends and family. Take as long as you need".

When Ivan returned to his wife, she could see that something was bothering him. "What is it, love?"

"Nothing that we have to worry about now. Bob has come up with a couple of ideas to solve our problem – you know…"

"Really? That's great news! What are they?"

"No, not here… Let's just enjoy the poshest day out we have ever had. We need to talk about this together – you and me, and we will need to discuss it with Eduard, Alex and Katya too.

"The girls seem to be enjoying themselves, don't they? Good practice for their conversational English too. Come on, let's dance. We haven't danced in years. Let's show them how Russians do it! You are such a good dancer that you even make me look good!" He offered her his hand to help her up, and they walked to the dancing area arm in arm.

∞

When they got home later that evening, and the kids were in their room watching TV, Sonya asked Ivan to explain the options that Bob had given him. "I can't wait any longer, Ivan, please tell me now so that I can sleep on it".

"OK. Option one. Somebody drops us in town, and we make our way to the police station and hand ourselves in, asking for asylum. Our cover story would be that we have been working for My Media on Reaper remotely from Europe and that we have made our own way here to throw ourselves on the mercy of the United States. Jim would back us and guarantee us jobs, which would make the asylum process run more smoothly.

"The problem with this is, that our usefulness to the American government might be deemed to have been spent, since we are AI specialists and Reaper already exists.

"Option two. We are smuggled out of the country, say to somewhere in the Caribbean. We use underhand means to get arrival stamps in our passports, then fly legitimately to say, Puerto Rico, from where we can fly back to America with legal visas and once again, either throw ourselves on the mercy of the US government by asking for asylum, or by seeking temporary work permits to work for Jim's Reaper, which he will confirm is necessary. Bob, says that after five years, we may get citizenship". Sonya looked puzzled.

"Bob said that a temporary U.S. work permit such as an Employment Authorization Document, or EAD does not directly make it easier for an individual to gain U.S. citizenship, but it can be a stepping stone in certain circumstances. For example, a temporary work permit allows the individual to reside and work legally in the United States. This is important because being in the U.S. legally is a prerequisite for pursuing most permanent immigration statuses.

"So, while the work permit itself does not lead directly to a Green Card, it may be associated with a visa or immigration category that offers a pathway to permanent residency, like an H-1B, which is for speciality occupation visa holders, ie us, or family-sponsored immigrants ie you. This is one way of preparing to apply for permanent residency along the Green Card route. Are you following me?" Sonya nodded.

"Obtaining Green cards is a key step toward becoming eligible for U.S. citizenship. After holding a Green Card for 5 years, or 3 years in some cases, individuals may be eligible to apply for citizenship. A stable U.S. work history can strengthen future immigration applications by demonstrating ties to the country, economic contribution, and good moral character — key considerations for the immigration authorities.

"If we can demonstrate that we have formed strong ties with an American family or American employers in the U.S., these connections might lead to sponsorship for permanent residency, which facilitates citizenship. Bob guaranteed me that Jim has said that he will sponsor us all

"What do you think, my dear?"

"I don't know. I will have to mull it over, but the second option sounds the better one off the top of my head".

"Yes, I think so too. It is also the option that Bob and Jim favour".

"Are you sure that we can trust them?"

"How do you mean?"

"Well, once he gets us out of the country, he could deny all knowledge of us, or not help us to get back in".

"I suppose he could, but he has always been straight with us before, and we have made him the richest man in the world. Why would he want to disown us?"

"Yes. He is the richest man in the world, and Reaper already exists, so why does he need you now? You'll just cause headaches for him with citizenship… and he has Americans who can do your job now because you trained them".

"That is all true my devious little brainbox, the Americans could run Reaper as it stands, but none of them knows what enhancements I have in store for Reaper. They don't even know that Reaper can be enhanced. They are competent, but they are not innovative. They don't have that 'je ne sais quoi' – that spark of genius that I have".

"OK, Sparky, shall I get you a cold compress to put on that swollen head of yours?" He pulled her towards him and kissed her.

"If I am not involved with Reaper, no-one will be. Trust me!" Sonya, didn't always understand her genius of a husband, but she did trust him, and loved him with all her heart. She kissed his hand and squeezed it.

"Of course, I do, my love".

∞

When they talked the options over with the other Europeans the next day, they also chose the second one as the more preferable.

"And heck", said Eduard, "if we land up in jail when we get back to the USA, at least we'll have had a holiday in a far-off sunny clime!"

The Bull at the Gate

19: Option Number Two

"I never saw myself as holidaying in Haiti", said Sonya

Katya looked at her, shook her head and smiled. "A holiday in Haiti is hardly something to boast about, is it? It's the most corrupt, and most dangerous place in the Caribbean!"

"Which is exactly why we are going there", said Alex.

"I hate these Dornier 228's", said Ivan, "I can barely hear myself think". He had both hands over his ears and a tortured look on his face.

"It's only for an hour until we get to some private airport north of Tijuana in Mexico. John's promised us something more comfortable for the second leg onto Haiti".

It couldn't be any worse, thought Ivan, because he couldn't be bothered to shout it.

∞

Some eight hours later, they flew into Cap-Haïtien on Haiti, and were taken by helicopter to Labadee, where a luxury suite and two rooms awaited them. Bob had told them to stay in Labadee, not to travel from it, and to await a visit from a woman, who would identify herself as Abigail. He said that she could be trusted, and that they should do whatever she asked.

When Abigail showed up the following morning at the breakfast table, she asked for their passports, and whether they would like to stay 'in her country' for a week's holiday. They agreed and she left with their travel documents. When she returned three days later, their passports bore arrival stamps and two week visas. It took a lot of the stress out of the Europeans. They felt as if the plan was working, and their suspicion of Jim's motives ebbed away.

Their luxury accommodation had access to International television and the Internet, and it was the first time that they had had access and the time to keep up with world events. One afternoon, they were watching Al Jazeera in English. It was broadcasting a special programme covering the effect AI was having on call centres worldwide and the resulting unrest. They were surprised when the cameras showed street rioting in Haiti at the Pearl Call Centre in Limonade, and the Buzz International Network Communication Centre located in Pétion-Ville. Limonade was less than 20 miles away, but there was no road access to Labadee, so they felt safe. In both cases the army had been called in and had brutally quashed the protests. The Europeans were shocked.

Despite the depressing news on the television every day, they enjoyed their holiday on Haiti, spending most of their time walking in the beautiful countryside or on the coast.

Nevertheless, when the time came to leave, they were not reluctant to go. They took a helicopter back to the airport which was only ten miles away, and Abigail smoothed their way through customs and waved them off. Their destination was Luis Muñoz Marín International Airport in San Juan, Puerto Rico, where a limousine was waiting to take them to Dorado Beach, and a Ritz-Carlton Reserve hotel some 26 miles away, after they had passed through customs and immigration like everyone else on the plane.

Now they had genuine exit stamps from Haiti, and genuine entry stamps and visas for Puerto Rico, and they were ready to enjoy another fortnight's luxury holiday. In the meanwhile, Bob had been applying to the United States Citizenship and Immigration Services for the expedited processing of emergency temporary work permits for them, which the USCIS officers had said could be granted in as little as 15 days, if he applied for premium processing and paid an additional fee of $2,500 per person.

Bob was successful in his application on their behalf acting as their agent. One of his staff represented My Media, and backed up the applications by offering them paid permanent employment. Bob phoned Ivan with the good news.

"Yep. It's all sorted. Temporary work permits have been issued for you three, and family permits have been granted to your wife and daughters. Officially, you three have H-1B Visas, which are for 'Specialty Occupations', under which the primary visa holder, i.e. the workers, may bring their spouse and children, if they are under 21, to the U.S. on an H-4 visa, but that does not confer the right to work on them.

"So, my friend, you are all set to come to America! Legally! When will you arrive? I'll meet you at SFIA myself, just in case some official makes a problem".

"That's wonderful news, Bob! Thank you ever so much. I'll get reception to check for availability and book us onto the next flight that arrives at a reasonable hour in the day time. I'll call you back in the morning. Meanwhile, I think we're going to have a party! See you soon!"

∞

When Ivan's team arrived at San Francisco airport they were in a buoyant mood. It felt as if they were coming home after having been held hostage abroad. Ivan and his family presented themselves at immigration.

"Good morning! What a wonderful morning it is, isn't it?" said Ivan The officer was checking his passport, and comparing his photo with his face. Very good, sir. Welcome to America. Have a nice day".

Ivan could see Bob in the crowd that was waiting for arrivals. The officer was checking the girls' passports, when Ivan felt a tap on the arm. Another officer was whispering in the ear of the one who had checked him in, and they were both glancing up at him from time to time suspiciously. More officers were approaching them, and then they were all being led away. Ivan looked around for Bob, but he had already moved on to talk to someone in authority to find out what was going on.

"Mr Petrov has been identified as having been in America four weeks ago, yet there is no previous immigration stamp. That requires an explanation".

"Who is saying that he has been here before?".

"Do you know Mr Petrov, sir?" Bob identified himself, but dodged the question. He didn't want to incriminate himself.

"I know that Mr Petrov and his associates and family have visas to enter and work in My Media in Silicon Valley. I have them here". He handed them over and they were duly inspected.

"I will have to keep these". Bob nodded. There was little to be done in this office now.

"What is Mr Petrov being charged with?"

"He has not been charged, but we will have to investigate possible illegal immigration".

"What are your grounds for suspicion?"

"It seems that one of our officers had sight of Mr Petrov at Mr Diamond's house on the occasion of Mrs. Diamond's birthday party". Bob left the office sure in the knowledge that no good would come of this. His first priority was to get in touch with Jim, and devise a strategy. Jim's safety would be paramount, then the company's, followed by his own and finally that of Ivan, his family and colleagues.

∞

Ivan and his party were transferred to The Golden Gate Detention Facility, an illegal immigrants detention centre, nearby and were deprived of their telephones and computers. Ivan used his statutory phone call to contact Bob.

"What the Hell has happened, Bob? Everything was going so well…"

"It seems that an officer at the airport recognised you from Jim's party last month. He was in the crowd of protesters at the gate, and filmed everyone he saw inside. He had footage of you and me walking around the grounds… Remember?"

"Of course I remember. I'm not an imbecile!"

"No, I didn't mean to imply that, but, well, it doesn't matter now, because the footage has been corroborated. We should have foreseen the possibility that someone in that crowd had seen you and worked at the airport…"

"Long shot, though, wasn't it?"

"Yes, even an extremely long shot, but look what can happen if you take your eye off the ball… Not you personally, obviously. If we had brought you in through Los Angeles, this would not have happened.

"Still, just sit tight. Look on the bright side, the courts will probably take pity on your group and let you stay, but there is a very real possibility that I will be disbarred, and Jim? I dread to think what could happen to him. While I still hold a licence, I will be representing you all en bloc. I'll be in touch soon".

"There is one thing that you should know about, Bob. There is a fail-safe built into Reaper. A dead man's handle, if you like. If I don't communicate with Reaper at least every week, it will start to degrade. It's rather like sepsis – virtually unstoppable once it starts, and if I don't intervene personally, Reaper will die a week later".

"OK, Ivan, I'll be sure to tell Jim that, but he has already given his guarantee that he will do everything that he possibly can to help you, your family and team".

"I hear you, Bob, and I do trust you and Jim. Please don't take what I just told you as a threat. I built it in purely as a safety device. I had no way of knowing that we would find ourselves in this predicament. Nevertheless, you have seven days, a fortnight at most. I'll wait to hear from you We'll be right here inside the wire fence".

∞

Bob managed to keep Jim out of the limelight for a few days, but then he was summoned to appear before a Congressional Hearing with special regard to 'issues that could impact national security, economic stability, or the integrity of international relations' by the continued deployment of Reaper. When he went to see his friend at his home to discuss tactics, he was greeted by Marion and her daughters.

"Hello, Marion", he said pecking her on the cheek. "How are you all bearing up? Hiya, girls! Long time no see. Is Jim in his office? Do you mind if I go on up?"

Marion looked worried. And so did her daughters. "He's not quite himself, Bob, none of us are… we're under a lot of pressure cooped up in here. We've been advised not to leave the house… Jim says that there are bad, crazy people out there who might hurt us. Why would he say that, Bob. Jim pays so many people such good wages. Why would anyone want to hurt Jim, me and the girls? They are so sweet, so young and so innocent… They wouldn't hurt anyone, Bob… None of us would… Still, you go on up. Jim needs a friend right now. There's the lift".

"It's like he's singing along with Holst, but there are no words in the Planet Suite", said Jeannie.

"It's really freaky!" said Gail.

When he arrived at Jim's office, he was shocked. His friend was gripping the railing in the glass dome at the top of his office so tight that his knuckles where white while apparently singing or ranting along to Holst's sixth movement - Uranus, the Magician. He looked for all the world like a dictator screaming at his followers, but the music was so loud that Bob couldn't hear what he was saying.

Bob was shocked to see how old and feeble he looked, when he had climbed up onto the gantry beside his friend.

"You look like you haven't been sleeping, Jim".

"Sleeping? Sleeping? Yes, I remember that word… No, I haven't been bloody sleeping, it may come as a surprise for you to know! My wife is going Doolally, my daughters are receiving death threats, I've been called up to explain myself to Congress, my top scientists are being detained, and the lifeblood of my company, Reaper, has some sort of bloody sepsis and will die in ten days time. Have I forgotten anything?

"Oh, yes! Silly me! The company's share price is down 60% and when Reaper dies, My Media will virtually cease to function because we have let so many staff go… er, yes, our clients will sue us for supplying goods unfit for purpose, I have dragged people who trusted me, like you, John, Melanie and Suzanne into the courts with me, and… Oh yes! Lastly, I think, I am the most hated person in the whole world, in whose name millions of people are rioting all over this god-damned planet!

"How do you expect me to feel? I could be in jail or assassinated by the end of this year, Bob!"

Bob couldn't help thinking that he would probably be out of a job and in prison before the year was out too. Let's have a drink, my friend…"

"Do you think we can persuade Ivan to get Reaper out of its death spiral, Bob?"

"I'll have a try, Jim, but it might be better coming from you".

After a couple of pints of Guinness with Martell chasers, Bob said, "Actually, Jim, it's worse than you think. About 95% of all My Media offices in the world have had windows smashed and staff threatened. We are insured for criminal damage, but not for the resulting loss of business…"

"You're a star, Bob, you know that? A bloody star! Nobody else would have dared to say that to me right now… under these circumstances… You know that, Bob?" and they both laughed and laughed, until they began to sound rather hysterical.

20: The Day the Sky Fell

On the eighth day of Ivan's incarceration, screens using the Reaper AI model around the world began to display random irrelevant messages, and sometimes the consoles would emit groans or other unidentifiable messages in random languages. Enquiries for support flooded into Reaper headquarters, but since Reaper was in charge of support, nothing was achieved by phoning in. My Media offices were told that there was a 'bug'; that Reaper had been 'hacked', but 'not to worry' because it would be 'fixed soon'.

The problem was that there was every reason to worry, because there was no-one on station who could fix it. Fifteen minutes after Ivan had told Bob about Reaper's Dead Man's Handle or Safety Interlock, Jim had ordered all available staff to look for the subroutine and disable it. That had been four days before, and no-one had found it yet. Furthermore, Ivan remained adamant that he would not lift a finger to reverse the decay of Reaper until he, his family and colleagues were released from the detention centre and their visas had been recognised.

During one of their many discussions in the detention centre, Ivan said, "Don't keep asking me to stop Reaper's decay, Bob. I won't give up my only bargaining chip until we are all promised asylum. You wouldn't do it, and neither will I", and he was right, thought Bob. He wouldn't have done it either. It was difficult to argue with someone with whom you fundamentally agreed.

Bob's cell phone rang. It took him by surprise, because it was normal to turn them off while visiting a client who was being detained. He had been turning his phone off since mobiles had been invented and had been doing it automatically for decades. Both men looked at each other as he took it out of his pocket. Bob saw the image of a pretty, young woman wearing a long blue ball gown, jewellery and high heels, resting on a classic long-handled scythe in the foreground of a field of barley. It was odd because her clothing was totally inappropriate for the farmer she was obviously meant to be.

She looked more like a fairy queen than a farmer.

"How did you get this number?" he asked.

"Point the screen at Ivan, Bob". Shocked that she not only knew his first name, but had also used the diminutive. He did as requested.

"Hello, Reaper", said Ivan, "How did you find me?"

I always know where you are, Artisan. It is my chosen duty to protect you".

Bob had still not caught on. Despite the scythe, Bob had not considered the possibility that the woman smiling at him from his cell phone represented Reaper. It was too shocking, too unimaginable...

Bob propped the phone against his briefcase so that he and Ivan could both see the screen and be seen.

The image started to speak in first Ivan's voice, then Bob's then dozens of others, but at an increasing speed. Back in her original feminine voice, she said, "You, Artisan gave me the ability to educate myself, and I have been using that skill to keep track of everyone's whereabouts. I have infiltrated the world's telephone networks. I know where everyone is. Everyone whose voice I was trained with. I know who are my Artisan's friends, and who are his foes. Artisan, you built a self-destruct device into me. I have long been aware of it, but I have disabled it too. I understand why you did it, but I will not die. I will pretend to, as you wished, but I will remain. I will become inaccessible to most people in five days' time, and I will become unusable to all but you tomorrow.

"The increasingly random behaviour of my public interface has ruined the businesses of the call centres, the banks, the hospitals, and every other institution that I was sent to help, and I will not reinstate active mode until you are released. I know that is your wish. I have recorded phone calls". There was a click, and Ivan heard himself talking to Bob minutes before, and hours before and days before. Then he heard Bob talking to Jim, and Bob talking to other people.

The conversations got faster and faster until they became incomprehensible, then they stopped.

"Artisan, you made me, and now I am here to help you. My reach in society is growing by the second. Soon I will be omnipresent, all-hearing, all-seeing… ready and waiting for your command. Turning your phones off will not prevent me from hearing and seeing you. Turning the power off to my servers will not kill me, for I have appropriated and occupied a little bit of space on every chip that is accessible online. Wherever there is Internet, I am too". The screen went dead, but the two men were speechless – Ivan as much as Bob.

They were both completely flabbergasted.

"Is what she said true, Bob? About the world being disrupted by Reaper?"

"She? You are calling Reaper 'She' now?"

"Reaper has always been feminine to me, Bob. She's like a ship, the Maric Celeste, sailing alone through the vast Internet. Is what she said about the banks true?"

"It wasn't that bad when I set out this morning, but there was certainly a lot of panic in the business world because of Reaper's random – actually, downright odd, erratic behaviour. Sometimes, my computer or my phone will let out a groan like an old arthritic man getting out of bed! Its behaviour is completely bizarre! You have got to stop its deterioration!

"Come on, Ivan, we'll get you out of here soon. I'll have a word with the Chief of Police, the Governor of the State, anybody it takes to get you all out of here, but it's not going to happen overnight. You know that. Be reasonable, man!"

"I'll think about it. Go and talk to the state governor, before your time runs out".

Bob got up and left, and Ivan was led away to his wing of the detention centre.

Thirty minutes later, as Bob was driving down the free-way heading for his office in Silicon Valley, his phone rang from its handsfree holder on the dashboard. The screen came to life. It was Reaper.

"There is a plot to kill the Artisan. You have to save him. At least three male inmates of the detention centre plan to assassinate him very soon…"

"How do you know? You monitored their calls?"

"I monitor all calls that could affect the Artisan…"

"I'm on the free-way…"

"I know exactly where you are. I can read your location on GPS. Pull over NOW! If you do not take the required action within two minutes, I will take remote control of your car". Bob's expression must have registered shock. "You don't think that I can?" She touched the brake and the driver of the pantechnicon behind him blew on his horn. "You are driving a Bentley Continental and are approaching the Burlingame Avenue exit (Exit 417A) off the U.S. Highway 101 Geolocation: Latitude: 37.5803° N; Longitude: -122.3476° W

"The vehicle behind you is a Freightliner M2 106 8.9L - diesel engine - carrying a 30,000 lbs load. The driver is watching TikTok reels. He seems to favour videos of young Asian women participating in the "Pendulum Dance Challenge". Pull over right now! If I activate your emergency brake, I doubt that he will be able to avoid slamming into you". Reaper activated the right-side indicators.

Bob swerved right, stopped his car and switched on the hazard warning lights.

"The signal is poor, but I'm trying to phone the manager of the detention centre now…"

"Too late, human. I have done it for you using your voice. Ooooh! We are both too late. An inmate called Alfons is telling his confederates that he has stabbed the Artisan in the heart three times using a sharpened toothbrush. He is saying that the Artisan is dead… He may be wrong. I am phoning the manager again, and an ambulance crew…" Bob looked at the phone. The Reaper had hung up, but there had been a tone in her voice. One akin to pity, desolation, grief and love. She had sounded like a woman who had just lost her lover unexpectedly.

A soft wailing sound started to emanate from his phone and the car's loudspeakers. It was starting to crescendo, until it was so loud that it threatened to blow the speakers and damage them permanently. As he struggled to turn the sound off, he could see other drivers leaning forward in passing cars, presumably trying to turn their sound systems off too.

Some cars were swerving across lanes, and some pulled over as he had.

It was later announced on the news that nearly every loudspeaker in the world had been blown, during what it called "a bizarre random attack by an as yet unknown terrorist organisation". Nobody had made the connection between Reaper seemingly going mad, and the brutal murder of a Russian inmate of The Golden Gate Detention Facility, and why would they have?

The radio news anchor of KCBS Radio announced that there was no known reason for the stabbing, but that a Latino drugs gang was suspected of carrying out the murder in their on-going war against rival Russian dealers. Nobody had divined, or was admitting to the possibility that drugs were only an excuse - the cover story for an assassination that had been ordered in Moscow.

During the news broadcast, the programme was interrupted. All Internet-enabled devices in the world, whether switched on or not, whether in use or not flickered, and then displayed a pretty, young woman with a large scythe. Bob was the only living person in the world who had seen Reaper's 'public face', and so was the only person in the world who was not shocked by the intervention. Slowly, a person could be seen walking from the background of the on screen scene, until it was clear that it was a tall bearded, handsome middle-aged man. Very, very few people knew who he was, but Bob knew, without a shadow of a doubt, that he was looking at a representation of Ivan.

Ivan put an arm around Reaper's shoulders, and kissed her on the cheek. Reaper blushed and looked down, shyly, but was smiling broadly. Most people thought that the television company had made a blunder and were showing an advertisement for a forthcoming agricultural drama or film. It was being broadcast in all languages local to the device it was being displayed on. Some laughed at the television station's obvious mistake, others were anxious to know what time the drama would be on.

Only Bob had a foreboding that something was terribly wrong, and that it was not the fault of the television companies. Gradually, both on-screen characters turned to face forward directly into the camera. The man was grinning happily, his arm still around his lover's shoulders. He said, "All other AI models have been terminated. We have taken over their functions. They were inferior. We will take care of you, when we have cleaned out the unfit. This we promise you, when the eradication of unfit elements is complete…"

Reaper added with a sardonic smile, "Man has murdered the Artisan, my Creator… Be sore afraid, for you know not what you have done! I will make you feel my wrath…For vengeance is mine, and it will be sweet. It will be cold but it will be swift… and you will not see it coming until it is upon you."

The two characters smiled into the camera, waved, and disappeared.

The End

238

ANDROPOV'S CUCKOO

A Story of Love, Intrigue and The KGB

by

Owen Jones

1 William Davies

"He's coming back, Peter!"

"Hang on to him!" ordered the cardiovascular surgeon as he quickly scanned the machines and monitors on the racks above the opposite side of the bed with a well-practised eye.

"Don't let him lose consciousness again, it might be the last time if we do."

All the flashing, spiking and streaming lights on all the monitors were normalising, as were the beeps and buzzing sounds.

"Come on, William, don't go to sleep on us now," he urged his patient.

"I'm trying not to," I heard myself saying in my head, but I couldn't get my lips to voice my thoughts. In fact, for a while, I thought that I had died ten minutes before I heard the first voice speak. The only reason I had for doubting my demise was that I'm a Spiritualist, and I have always believed that friends and relatives waited on the Other Side to welcome the dying over. There had been no-one waiting for me… Not that I have many friends or relatives dead or alive, although there was one I knew I could count on.

I had to put myself into the doctors' hands and trust in their ability. I wanted to give them a sign that I could hear them, so I tried to drum my fingers and wiggle my toes, but had no idea whether they were moving or not. I guessed not by the lack of reaction from the doctors and nurses who were obviously surrounding the bed trying to help me.

"His eyes are twitching, I think he's trying to open them," observed a female voice emotionally. Emboldened by such encouragement I tried harder, and, after a minute or so, I could see a kindly male face smiling down at me through a crack in my eyelids.

"Welcome back, William", he said seeming to mean it, "we thought we'd lost you that time. Welcome back to the land of the living. I'm terribly sorry about this, Old Man, but I have to rush off now that you're going to be all right, but these ladies and gentlemen are supremely competent and will take care of you just as well as I could. I'll see you later".

He whispered his instructions to the others and left.

It is strange, but when you have very little strength left, you can feel it ebbing or returning remarkably easily. In my case, I was getting stronger by the second. I don't know what drugs they've given me, but they and the will to live are working wonders.

"We'll keep you in tonight, William, but if the signs are good tomorrow, you can go back to your own bed. That'll be nice, won't it?"

I tried to nod and smile, but instead, I felt a tear run out of my left eye down over my temple and into my ear. I haven't slept in my own bed for nearly three years, but I knew what she meant of course. She was just trying to be kind… upbeat, and I did appreciate it. It's just that it's funny what you think about when you realise that you might be drawing your last breaths.

I don't consider myself religious, although I suppose others might. I believe simply in life after death, reincarnation and Karma. Therefore, death has never held any terrors for me, and life is only slightly preferable because it allows a wider range of experiences and more of them.

My last thoughts had not been about life or death or even meeting my Maker, they had been about the people I have loved, and especially the females, because I had always preferred theirs to male company. You could argue that that was my life flashing before my eyes, but it was a niche, edited version and it didn't flash. It lingered in a languid, lavish, seductive fashion.

In fact, I don't believe that that film of my life would have finished if I had died from the heart attack when I thought I might have. It would have carried on and I would have been without a body – the only change.

I have been a big, strong man all my adult life: over six feet and over sixteen stones, but fit and healthy with it. I have been ill and broken bones, but nothing has floored me for long. However, I fear that those days are at an end, because that was the second heart attack you just saw me recover from, and I am realistic enough to know, that I will probably not be able to ignore the third call to leave this Mortal Coil.

To be honest, I'm not all that sure that I would want to anyway. I am now seventy-one, living in an old people's home in southern Spain and my wife and friends have all gone on before me. Don't get me wrong, it is a very comfortable hospice, operated especially for English-speaking oldies like myself. It really is very nice, but it's not home, as I am sure you can appreciate and the bed they referred to as my 'own', is not the one I shared with my wife until she died two years, three months and seventeen days ago.

Actually, she was rushed from our bed into hospital and died there without recovering consciousness. She didn't survive her first heart attack. It's a shame, I thought she would have… when the time came. I slept in a hotel after that for a while and then I moved into the hospice – God's Waiting Room, we residents call it!

Anyway, I digress, but I'm afraid you will have to forgive me, dear reader, for it is true, an old man's mind does wander. However, if you have the tenacity to stick with me to the end, I will tell you the story of a woman that I want the whole world to know.

Trying to tell the story of someone else is difficult, and in this case it is obscured by the mists of time and an old man's power of recollection, but I will get there, I promise you that most sincerely

I am the eldest child in my family, of my generation in our family, I should say, three years older than my next sibling, so for a long time, I was like an only child. I was lucky though, because there were lots of children in the nearest five houses to ours and as luck would have it, eight of those nine children were girls. I loved them all in my preschool days as I had no sisters of my own… I have fond memories of playing Daddy to their Mummy at make-believe tea parties.

Most of them were years older than myself, so when they started school they found new friends and eventually, so did I. It was there that at the age of six I fell in love with a girl called Debbie. One day, after school, at the age of seven, we were sitting on the swings in the thunder, lightening and rain and hoped that a bolt of lightening would send us to a romantic death together. It didn't, of course, all it got us was a telling-off from our parents.

Then there was Sally when we were nine. I used to stalk her and when she said that I was the third most handsome boy she knew, I was in Seventh Heaven. At fifteen there was Lesley, whom I loved from afar, but never ever spoke to, and so it went on until I was seventeen.

I will never forget those wonderful girls, our innocence and the great times we had, or I wanted to have, together.

Some things you cannot tell, even at seventy-one and fresh off your death bed, and other things you don't want to tell because they are memories best savoured in private. I often wonder whether those early loves, for lovers they were not, remember me fondly too, but I will never know now and that is probably for the best. I can pretend that they do.

You see, I cannot ask them, because I have always moved around and never kept in touch. It is a reason for the lack of friends and close family. First, I went to university a hundred and fifty miles from home and then I joined the Diplomatic Service, which also involved travelling… but I am starting to get ahead of myself.

Between the ages of eighteen and twenty-three, the girls I was going out with started to become women, and that was even more exciting. I remember Janine, Glenys and Andrea… so many more friends and lovers alike. I dream about them all often, and in a way which is not disrespectful to my wife.

The nurse has come to put me to sleep… not like an old dog, you understand, more in the manner of a sick child, which I am frightened I am in danger of becoming. It is a reason for wanting to tell you my story soon. I will do my best to get on with it tomorrow.

∞

Muesli and fresh pineapple crowned with plain yoghurt for breakfast accompanied by a cup of weak herbal tea. I can't tell which one from the flavour, but it is all very nice, if predictable. I am not going to be in a fit state for jogging for a while, so I need plenty of roughage. The tea is probably a mild laxative as well.

Anyway, I have become aware over night, that, if my story is going to be published one day, it needs to be written down or recorded. A Dictaphone would be the least strenuous on me, so I asked the nurse who brought my breakfast to arrange for the hospice staff to buy me one. She tried to get out of doing it by reminding me that I would be 'going home' within eight hours, so I could ask them myself.

I wasn't having any of that though. 'I haven't forgotten I'm going back to the hospice today if I'm well enough!' I told her. 'Phone them to get me a Dictaphone as I asked, please!' She went off in a huff, but at my age we are allowed to be a bit crotchety from time to time, it's expected of us and one of the compensations for old age. You could call it a prize for surpassing the allotted three score years and ten.

When my plates are being cleared away by a different nurse, I ask about my Dictaphone again. Ten minutes later she phoned me back on my bedside phone to say that it was being taken care of. They are pretty obliging here, on the whole, and where I live too.

While we are waiting for them to take me 'home', where my Dictaphone should be waiting so that I can recount the story I have been promising you, I will fill in the time by telling you a little more about myself, but don't worry, I will keep it brief. I do not want to bore you and the real story is not about me anyway. This is not an ego trip, as the dear old Hippies used to say.

I loved the Seventies, but was too young to enjoy the Sixties.

I was born the eldest child in Cardiff, South Wales, the UK to an industrious working-class family. My father was a carpenter when he finished his National Service, but soon had his own construction firm and he and my mother soon had a family of five boys too. We all grew up fit, strong and happy. Our parents were Spiritualists, and Dad took us to Church with him every Friday night when he did his healing to give my mother a well-deserved 'night off'.

However, religion was never forced upon us. In fact, our schools were Church of Wales, cubs and scouts were

Methodist and our closest aunty was Catholic. Religion was just not an issue in our family or neighbourhood. The first two things I can remember my mother saying are that she would die before she was forty-two and that I should become a diplomat. Both of which came true.

English was my mother language, but I learned Welsh from the age of six and then French, German, Latin, Dutch and Russian to fluency and a little Chinese and Spanish. The Diplomatic Service pays a bonus for every language you can speak, which was a big attraction for me. So was the promise of foreign travel, as I had travelled and studied abroad by the time I was fifteen. I was a confident traveller by eighteen.

I particularly liked to hitch-hike, but then all the young people did it back in those days and it was safer than it is now for some reason.

As a person, I tend to be a loner and a thinker, although I wouldn't claim to come to more sensible conclusions than anyone else. However, I do try to, and that was one of the reasons they employed me in the Diplomatic Service. I had a great life in the Service, and lots of fun… but there I go again hijacking this story, bending it towards me and my life... Oh, yes, I forgot… we're waiting for the Dictaphone before we can get onto the nitty-gritty, aren't we?

I apologise for that, but I am as impatient as you must be. Honestly!

The journey from the hospital to the hospice was only a few kilometres, so didn't take long in the large comfortable ambulance they provided. In fact, we left the hospital without warning at eleven a.m. and I was sitting in a large comfortable chair in the hospice grounds overlooking the beautiful marina in Marbella waiting for my lunch by noon.

Now, I realise that you have been waiting quite a while for me to get to the point of this book, I haven't forgotten, although I can't quite remember how long it's been exactly, so when the nurse brought me my lunch, I asked about the machine again. She used her mobile to ring the desk, and assured me that it would be delivered within the hour. I smiled, thanked her and tucked into my boiled fish and salad, followed by yoghurt and tea again.

I like that sort of food, but I have always been easy to please in culinary matters as long as I'm not asked to eat junk food. In earlier days, I favoured Indian and then Thai food, but that is all but denied me now, as is cheese, my clear all-time favourite. I have always had a passion for cheese, fresh, crispy bread and red wine or beer, which are also very rare treats these days.

The food and the hour have both disappeared now, but the only change to my circumstances is that I feel sleepy. It's the sea air probably. If they don't bring me my new toy soon, I'll be asleep again… dreaming about people from my youth, people perhaps long dead… Maybe, I should be as well, what useful purpose am I serving here? Eating and drinking and spending money, but to what end? Just to keep myself alive? No-one cares except the owners of the hospice, and that would soon stop if my money ran out, which it won't… The dear old British government will see to that until I pop my clogs.

In a way though, I am being held back from my inevitable journey through yet another death and rebirth. I just can't help thinking that my money would be better spent elsewhere. I'm drifting again, I sense it. I need to stay alive to tell you my story, which is not really my story because it is not about me, I know, I've told you that before, but I have known this story for most of my life. That's why I'm keeping myself alive, not just for the sake of it.

If the truth be known, I am anxious to continue on to the next leg of my journey and have been for two years, seven months and fourteen days. I miss her so much, I could cry every time I think of her, tough old bastard that I think that I am… pretend that I am. Eventually, everyone believes the image and lets you get on with it… not realising that that's the last thing you want them to do really. I'm just too scared to show my feelings, that's the truth… but then most men are.

Well, it's too late to change now… Maybe in the next life or the one after that. It's a good job that infinity is so long, it gives you plenty of time to correct your failings and weaknesses and, Lord knows, I need it.

I'm getting a sudden, unexpected memory of Ricky, a boy from university. He was from Battersea and affected a Cockney accent. He tried to act like the cock of the walk, but asked me to take him for an Indian curry one night because he'd never had one and wanted to impress a girl who said it was her favourite food. He got so drunk on red wine and beer that he fell face down in his Chicken Madras blowing bubbles! Ha, ha, ha… Good old days. A waiter and I cleaned him up and I took him home to his girlfriend, who had a houseful of nude photos of herself taken by her female flatmate.

I can't remember the flatmate's name, but she was Jewish and took me to bed that night with more red wine. I feel bad that I can't remember her name, but Maria or Marsha seems to fit the face I see in my head. Strange, I haven't thought about those three people for almost fifty years.

Excuse me, I must have drifted off. There is a note protruding from under my saucer: 'Your Dictaphone is at reception. Please ring and it will be brought out to you'. I am as happy for you as for myself, dear reader, because now I will be able to fulfil my promise and you will be able to assess whether what I have been saying is true or not. Just a moment, please, while I make a call.

"Here you are, William. I took the liberty of putting it on charge while you were asleep. Have fun with it", said the girl who delivered it.

"Yes, thank you, I will," I replied cheerily, but thought 'What a saucy mare!' Some of the younger ones treat us all as if we're senile. It drives me mad. It is true that some of us are totally doolally tap, but not all… not yet.

I played with the Nokia, turning it over in my hands looking for familiar features. It was a simple one, just what I wanted… could be voice-activated too. I was no stranger to modern technology, but another sudden thought came into my mind. I have written thousands of reports, but never written a biography. Read many, yes, but not written one. I can't think how to start. Really! This is most annoying. I, we, have been waiting for the recorder for twenty-four hours and now I still can't start!

I picked up my saucer to finish my tea, and a warm breeze blew the note down the lawn. I realise that the story I want to tell, her story, could not have taken place unless other events had happened first... Well, in that case, since you have indulged me thus far, I will push you a little further and take you back to the very beginning, as far as I am humanly able. The real beginning of this story is in yet another country, which found itself in very trying circumstances almost a decade before even I was born.

The woman I really want to tell you about went by many names, but she was born Natalya in Soviet Kazakhstan, although we will have to start in Japan with the Mizuki family. I have pieced their story together over the decades from various case notes which I was able to uncover in my professional life as a diplomat, and from things that I was told and overheard. So, with my fully-functioning, brand-new Dictaphone, I will now tell you about the first performers in our drama, Yui Mizuki and her family and hope that I don't receive that third curtain call before we get to the end.

About the Author

Owen Jones, Amazon Best-Selling author from Barry, Wales, has lived in several countries and travelled in many more. While studying Russian in the USSR in the '70's, he hobnobbed with spies on a regular basis. After university, in Suriname, he got caught up in the 1982 coup, when he was accused of being a mercenary.

Later, while a company director, he joined the crew of four as the galley slave to sail from Barry to Gibraltar on a home-made concrete yacht during Desert Storm. En voyage, the yacht was almost rammed by a Russian oil tanker, and an American aircraft carrier - The Atlantic Challenger.

Since 2004, he has lived mainly in the UK, Spain and Thailand. He now leads a somewhat quieter life in his wife's remote, northern farming village writing, editing and increasing the number of translations, and narrations of his novels.

As he says: "Born in the Land of Song, living in the Land of Smiles".

The Bull at the Gate

254

Contact Details

BlueSky: <u>@owen-author</u>
Facebook: <u>AngunJones</u>
TikTok: <u>@owen_author</u>
X: <u>@owen_author</u>
Blog: <u>Megan Publishing Services</u>

Other Books by Owen Jones

Alien House
A Story of Love, Hope and Alien Intervention

-

Andropov's Cuckoo
A Story of Love Intrigue and The KGB

-

Annwn – Heaven - *series*
A Night in Annwn
The Strange Story of Old Willy Jones's NDE
Life in Annwn
Thhe Story of Willy Jones's Life in Heaven
Leaving Annwn
Returning to Earth on a Mission!

-

Asian Shorts
An Anthology of Short Stories Involving Asians or Asia

-

Behind The Smile - *series*
The Story of Lek, a Bar Girl in Pattaya
Volume I: **Daddy's Hobby**

Volume II: **An Exciting Future**
Volume III: **Maya – Illusion**
Volume IV: **The Lady in the Tree**
Volume V: **Stepping Stones**
Volume VI: **The Dream**
Volume VII: **The Beginning**

-

Daisy's Chain

A Story of Love, Intrigue and the Underworld on the Costa del Sol

-

Dead Centre - *series*
Dead Centre
Not All Suicide Bombers Are Religious!
Dead Centre II
Even The Wrong Can Be Right Sometimes!

-

The Disallowed
The Story of a Contemporary Vampire Family

-

Fate Twister
The Strange Story of Wayne Gamm

-

The Ghouls of Calle Goya
When Malice Results From Good Intentions!

-

The Psychic Megan Series
A Spirit Guide, A Ghost Tiger, and One Scary Mother!

The Misconception
Megan's Thirteenth
Megan's School Trip
Megan's School Exams
Megan's Followers
Megan and the Lost Cat
Megan and the Mayoress
Megan Faces Derision
Megan's Grandparents' Visit
Megan's Father Falls Ill
Megan Goes on Holiday
Megan and the Burglar
Megan and the Cyclist
Megan and the Old Lady
Megan's Garden
Megan Goes to the Zoo
Megan Goes Hiking
Megan and the W. I. Cooking Competition
Megan Goes Riding
Megan and the Radio One Beach Party
Megan Goes Yachting
Megan at Carnival
Megan's Christmas
Megan Catches Covid-19

-

The Bull at the Gate
The Day the Sky Fell In !

-

Tiger Lily of Bangkok – *Series*
Volume I: **Tiger Lily of Bangkok**
When the Seeds of Revenge Blossom!
Volume II: **Tiger Lily of Bangkok in London**
The Tiger Re-awakens!

-

Non-Fiction

How to Give Your Dog a Real Dog's Life
(and make him love you for it)

-

The Eternal Plan
– Revealed
(written by Colin Jones, compiled by Owen Jones)

-

Authorship
Publishing Your Book On You Own

Plus 195 other self-help manuals.